take a chance on me

take a chance on me

gossip girl
the carlyles

Created by
Cecily von Ziegesar

Written by
Annabelle Vestry

poppy

LITTLE, BROWN AND COMPANY
New York   Boston

Poppy
Hachette Book Group
237 Park Avenue, New York, NY 10017
Visit our Web site at www.pickapoppy.com

Poppy is an imprint of Little, Brown Books for Young Readers.
The Poppy name and logo are trademarks of Hachette Book Group, Inc.

First Edition: May 2009

The characters, events, and locations in this book are fictitious. Any similarity to
real persons, living or dead, is coincidental and not intended by the author.

alloyentertainment
Produced by Alloy Entertainment
151 West 26th Street, New York, NY 10001

Cover design by Andrea C. Uva
Cover photo by Roger Moenks

ISBN 978-0-316-02066-4
10 9 8 7 6 5 4 3 2 1
CWO

Printed in the United States of America

Gossip Girl novels created by Cecily von Ziegesar:

We know what we are, but know not what we may be.

—Hamlet, William Shakespeare

gossipgirl.net

topics   sightings   your e-mail   post a question

hey people!

It's mid-October, otherwise known as Indian summer—the schizophrenic time of year when girls wear their favorite Alice + Olivia frocks layered over their wool Tibi leggings, when coffee orders suddenly switch from iced to hot, and when certain people (you know who you are) *still* think it's acceptable to bust out their Malia Mills bikinis and sunbathe in Sheep Meadow on weekend afternoons, hoping the pickup soccer game–playing St. Jude's boys might notice.

According to historical legend, Indian summer was known as the time of year when tensions were *especially* high between natives and new-comers. And here on the Upper East Side, history seems to be repeat-ing itself. Case in point? **O** and **R,** the former best guy buddies whose city bromance was one for the books, swam together, ran together, drank together—they seemed inseparable. And they were . . . until **R** caught **O** hooking up with his girlfriend. **O** got a bloody nose . . . and the girl. Now that **O** has completely stolen **K** from **R**, the two won't so much as talk. Sad. I guess sharing isn't caring, after all.

And that's not the only skirmish we've witnessed this fall. The freckly-faced ballerina **J** and socialite-in-training **A** have already had territo-rial battles over everything from couture to classmate loyalty. And even though **A** seemingly gained ground when her sister **B** dated **J**'s ex, now **B** is flying solo and **A** is *fighting* solo. Good thing **A** is going to be spending her afternoons safely ensconced within glass-walled offices for her highly coveted media internship. And since **J**'s back with her boyfriend, maybe she can forgive and forget. Miracles *can* happen, right? And not just on Thirty-fourth Street?

So what to do if you're feeling a chill in the air that's *not* related to a dropping thermostat—one that can't be fixed by your new DVF A-line herringbone coat? Well, why not take a cue from one sparkly-eyed bohemian nymph and skip town? **B** has been avoiding stateside drama in favor of exploring the beaches, shops, and cafes of the Spanish seaside in Barcelona—solo. Is she second-guessing her hasty breakup with a certain Manhattan mogul-in-training, doing some soul searching, or looking for a certain Spanish boy who was recently visiting NYC? One thing's for sure: She may be single, but she's not alone. She's been spotted all over Barcelona, constantly trailed by an army of admirers. Some girls have all the luck!

sightings

A at a newsstand on Seventy-second and Lex, picking up copies of *Vogue*, French *Vogue*, Italian *Vogue*, *Harper's*, and *Tatler.* Boning up on the competition before her big *Metropolitan* internship? Or just making a really ambitious collage? . . . **O** and **K** making out next to a rack of chips at a bodega on Madison and Sixty-second. And on a bench in Central Park. And on the downtown 6 train. Either these lovers don't know about secluded rooftop terraces, or they seriously get off on PDA. . . . The recently reunited **J** and **J.P.**, sharing an Evian at **Corner Bakery** on Ninety-third, with **J.P.**'s three puggles in tow. **R** throwing dozens of ripped-up photographs into the East River, crying the whole time. Brings new meaning to drowning your sorrows . . . And a smiling **B**, on La Rambla in Barcelona, being catcalled by everyone in her path. Hola, bebé!

your e-mail

q: Chismosa,
I have heard a rumor of a beautiful brown-haired girl in Barcelona, looking for a man she met in New York. I believe that was me. Please to tell her that I am in Majorca, on my submarine, and I would love to see her.
—Latin Lover

a: Dear LL,
Sadly, I don't know where your tousled bohemian beauty is either, but we're hoping she comes home soon.
—GG

q: Dear GG,
I'm a senior at Barnard and I was supposed to score this amazing internship at *Metropolitan*, the legendary New York fashion mag that totally propelled the career of anyone who's anyone in the industry? And suddenly I hear some girl who's a junior in *high school* scored the internship? WTF? I guarantee you she doesn't even know her Joan Didion from her Mary McCarthy. What's wrong with this world? Seriously, I'm just about ready to give up on New York.
—editennui

a: Dear EE,
Unfortunately, sometimes it really *is* who you know, so maybe this girl had some legendary connections. But look on the bright side: Perhaps you don't want to know those people anyway?
—GG

clothes call

These are strange days, where one morning it feels like you should be sunning in Sagaponack rather than slaving away at pre-calc, and the next it's back to frigid. For my part, I'm off to Barneys to stock up on cozy TSE cashmere cardigans. You may not be able to control public opinion, but you *can* control your own comfort. No matter how cold it gets—or how icy your former besties are acting—don't let it stop you from being hot.

You know you love me,

gossip girl

the love you make is equal to the love you take

"Ow!" Owen Carlyle grunted as a bagel hit him, hard, square in the center of his broad shoulders. He whirled around and furrowed his blond eyebrows at the swimmers hanging out on the steps of the Y. Scrawny Chadwick Jenkins and linebacker-size Ken Williams smiled back at him angelically, as if they were choirboys at St. Patrick's Cathedral rather than testosterone-laced high schoolers.

"Quit it, okay?" Owen grumbled, looking away from them and toward the gridlocked Second Avenue traffic. Owen was all for swim team bonding, particularly before their first meet of the season. But it was a little embarrassing to be surrounded by these guys when they were acting like Ritalin-pumped kindergarteners. Especially when his new girlfriend, Kelsey, was supposed to meet him any moment.

"Hey baby."

Owen whirled around and saw Kelsey walking toward him. It had been pouring all morning, but by early afternoon the rain had finally devolved into a misty light drizzle. Kelsey's strawberry blond hair was slightly damp, as if she'd toweled off after a shower, and her pink rubber rain boots matched her fitted pink trench coat, belted loosely at her tiny waist. From a distance, it looked like she wasn't wearing anything underneath. Owen's mind started to work overtime.

Right, *just* his mind.

Every time he saw Kelsey, Owen's heart thudded hard in his chest. He'd felt it ever since he first saw her, back in July, at a party in Nantucket. He'd been hanging at the outskirts of one of the typical summer beach parties, and she'd come with some friends from the Cape, on vacation from New York. They'd seen each other at the same time, and by the end of the night, they'd wound up on the other side of the beach, losing their virginities to each other. It was kind of wild, but also the most romantic night of Owen's life. When he moved to New York a couple months later, he kept hoping to run into her. And in a ridiculous twist of fate, he had. On the first day of school Rhys Sterling, the St. Jude's swim team captain and Owen's new friend, introduced Owen to Kelsey—as his *girlfriend*. A few weeks and one bloody nose later, Owen had lost a friend and gained a girlfriend. He'd never been happier.

Or more Shakespearian?

Kelsey tapped Owen on the temple with a slim, pale peach–polished fingernail. "Hello?" she asked, acting mock-hurt at his spaciness.

"Sorry!" Owen quickly tore his thoughts away from fantasy Kelsey. The real thing was so much better. He pulled her to him, rubbing his hands up and down her back. He planted his mouth lightly on hers. Her lip gloss tasted like Swedish fish.

Behind them, the guys started whistling and cheering. Owen reluctantly broke apart from Kelsey and glared at his teammates.

"God, you guys are so lame," Kelsey called out good-naturedly, sticking out her tongue at the team. Owen kept grinning like an idiot. When Kelsey was here, everything was just *better*. Of course, there was the ever-present nagging feeling of guilt that he'd totally screwed up his best friend's life.

There's always something. . . .

"I missed you today. I was thinking about you," Kelsey whispered, playing with a delicate silver flower-shaped necklace that landed in the center of her chest. Drops of rain gave her skin a dewy, glowy look, and Owen wished they were in his flannel-covered bed instead of the middle of the street. He tore his gaze away from the hint of cleavage and instead locked it on her coral-colored lips. God, she was sexy.

He pulled Kelsey closely to him again, nuzzling his nose into the top of her honey-colored, slightly damp hair.

"Fresh roasted nuts!" the street vendor on the corner hawked. Behind him, the swim team guys snickered as if it was the most amusing thing they'd ever heard. Owen pulled away from Kelsey in frustration.

"Let's take a walk," he suggested, flicking his gaze back and forth as if he were a spy on lookout. Ninety-second Street was pretty empty, with only one woman hurriedly walking her slobbering black Lab past each fenced-in tree.

"Okay. But I don't want you to be late to the meet." Kelsey bit her lip. Owen smiled, loving how concerned she was. It was nice to feel taken care of.

"I won't be," he said definitively, wrapping his fingers around her wrist. He caressed the well-worn silver surface of her Tiffany ID bracelet, memorizing the grooves in the loopily engraved letters KAT. It was the bracelet Kelsey had left on the Nantucket beach that summer. Owen had brought it to New York with him and used to sleep with it under his pillow, trying to somehow conjure Kat, his dream girl. He hadn't known then that K. A. T. were her initials: Kelsey Addison Talmadge. The mystery behind her name somehow suited her, the way she'd just *appeared* in his life.

As soon as they rounded the corner, out of sight of the swim team boys, he gently pushed Kelsey against the redbrick wall of the Y and leaned in to kiss her. He didn't even care if it was in broad daylight. After weeks of having to keep their desire a secret, he and Kelsey could *finally* be together. He could feel her long eyelashes against his cheek and she just felt so *good* and—

"Classy, Carlyle!" A voice interrupted Owen's reverie. He broke away from Kelsey, wiping his mouth self-consciously with the back of his hand. Walking up the street, jauntily swinging his maroon Speedo St. Jude's swim team bag in one hand and stroking a full blond beard with the other, was Hugh Moore, a fellow junior and varsity swimmer. While all the swim team guys had grown ridiculous facial hair as part of a pact, Hugh was the only member who hadn't eventually shaved. He'd kept the beard because it made him look a few years older and got him into the divey bars that peppered Second Avenue without an ID.

"Hey Hugh," Owen mumbled, and turned back to Kelsey. He ran his fingers through Kelsey's hair and leaned in toward her. He kissed her neck and held the small of her back, not caring if Hugh was there, probably recording the whole thing on his iPhone to upload to YouTube. Perv. He pressed his body against hers, and she pressed eagerly back. They were kissing passionately, and Owen had practically forgotten where he was, when he heard an awkward throat-clearing sound from Hugh. Annoyed, he looked up.

There, rounding the corner, was Rhys Sterling. His maroon St. Jude's blazer was wrinkled and his face looked drawn and gray. His broad shoulders were slumped, and he didn't even try to avoid the puddles of rain on the sidewalk.

Hugh doubled back and clapped a hand on Rhys's shoulder, propelling him past Owen and Kelsey. "Ready to kick Oriole ass, dude?" Hugh asked jovially.

Rhys squirmed away from Hugh's meaty hand and stood, rooted to the sidewalk. He knew Hugh was trying to distract him from the scene in front of him. As if he could possibly forget what he'd seen: his former girlfriend and his former friend, together. Kelsey's strawberry blond hair tumbled down her back, and she was smiling. It felt like she was smiling just to spite him.

"Ready to *rock*?" Hugh repeated, clearly sensing Rhys's discomfort. He offered his hand for a high five. Rhys awkwardly tried to slap it, as if he couldn't care less that his ex-girlfriend and his ex–best friend were practically having *sex* on the sidewalk.

"Hugh, we're running late," Rhys announced in an artificially loud voice, just because he didn't know what the hell else to say. As soon as he heard his words, he cringed. He sounded like a neurotic soccer mom. He squinted down at the ground, forcing himself to move one John Varvatos limited edition shoe in front of the other. Maybe he should just keep walking until he reached Canada, or any other goddamn place where he wouldn't be reminded of how his girlfriend—the person he'd loved more than anyone in the world—had taken him for a fucking fool and betrayed him.

"Rhys?" Kelsey turned toward him, her large, ocean-blue eyes pleading.

"I'm not talking to you, Kelsey," Rhys spat angrily. He cringed. *That* was the best he could come up with? He wanted to kick himself as he trudged toward the door of the Y, avoiding eye contact with Owen.

"I should . . ." Owen shrugged apologetically as he let go of Kelsey's hand.

"I'll see you later. If you win, I might have an extra-special surprise for you," Kelsey teased, her eyes gleaming. Owen grinned from ear to ear, the guilt almost gone.

Out with the old, in with the . . . lewd?

a is for intern

"Fuck!" Avery Carlyle exclaimed as she stepped into a huge puddle outside the Dennen Publishing Enterprises building after school on Friday. It was the first day of her internship at *Metropolitan*, the legendary city-centric fashion magazine, and now her new naughty secretary–style black seamed Wolford stockings were soaked to the ankle, and her vintage Prada T-strap pumps squeaked with every step she took.

The Dennen Publishing Tower, opposite Grand Central, was a brand-new art deco–inspired architectural wonder that fit seamlessly into the New York landscape. Skinny women in towering Jimmy Choos and chunky Stella McCartney boots were clustered outside the row of revolving glass doors, sucking on Parliaments as they barked into their BlackBerries. Messengers hopped off bikes, their arms laden with heavy bags and packages, while a convoy of shiny black town cars waited patiently at the curb.

Avery took a deep breath and pushed nervously through a revolving door. Today was the first day of the rest of her new and improved life. She'd had a bit of a shaky start in the city: She'd immediately found herself the enemy of Jack Laurent, the bitchi-est, vainest, most insecure girl in the junior class. Then Avery had won a highly coveted school leadership position only to discover it required weekly meetings with the Constance Billard board of overseers, who were really just a group of also bitchy, possibly alcoholic octogenarians.

But, Avery reminded herself as she patted the thick black and silver Marc Jacobs headband perched atop her wheat-blond hair, her luck seemed to be changing. Ticky Bensimmon-Heart—the world-famous editor in chief of *Metropolitan*—was on the Con-stance overseers' board and had rescued Avery by offering her an internship at the prestigious magazine. Soon, all of the New York media world would love Avery, and Jack Laurent and her bitchy posse would wet their pants in jealousy.

She marched up to the marble-topped security desk in the corner. A bored, white-haired guy looked her up and down.

For security purposes only.

"Avery Carlyle. I'm here for *Metropolitan*," she said in her most professional voice. The impressive lobby had waterfalls flanking the escalators and gorgeous white marble floors, and she sup-pressed the urge to twirl around, *Funny Face* style.

"ID?" the security guard asked in a bored voice, oblivious to the moment Avery was having. She fished for her Massachusetts driver's license in the brand-new Hermès bag she'd bought in Soho this weekend as a starting-work present.

"Good luck." The security guard winked as he handed her a dorky visitor's pass sticker. "Floor thirty-five. Top of the heap. Make sure to wear the pass until we get you a permanent one."

Avery slapped the sticker on her skirt, where she could cam-ouflage it with her bag—no way was she going to wear it like a dorky name tag. She followed the herd of gazelle-like girls up the escalator and toward the elevator banks, pretending to know where she was going. On floor thirty-five, the elevator opened into an all-white reception area decorated with huge, blown-up photos of *Metropolitan*'s most famous covers. Avery stared at the images of Andy Warhol, Edie Sedgwick, and Jackie Kennedy. She sucked in a deep breath. She was *in*.

"May I help you?" The girl sitting behind the desk didn't bother to look up from her gleaming white iMac. She had straight black hair that landed halfway down her back and thick bangs that skimmed her eyes. She looked like Angelina Jolie in her goth, vial of blood–wearing years.

"I'm here to see Ticky Bensimmon-Heart," Avery announced, pleased with how official that sounded. She was even more excited than she'd been on her first day at school.

And remember how well *that* day turned out?

"Who are you?" The Angelina look-alike looked up from her computer.

Avery smiled her best first-day-of-work smile and squared her shoulders. The photograph of Jackie seemed to be smiling at her. "Avery Carlyle?" She hated how it came out like a question. "Avery *Carlyle*," she said again, emphasizing her last name. "I'm the intern," she added.

"You're an intern," she repeated, the way she might have said, *You're a garbage truck driver*, or *You're a proctologist*. "You're not seeing Ticky, trust me. I'll call McKenna to fetch you. She's the intern wrangler."

Avery furrowed her eyebrows. Intern *wrangler*? What did they think she was, a farm animal?

Avery perched on the black leather couch and flipped through the latest issue of the magazine. A fashion spread featured models lying languorously on the Brooklyn Bridge, about to get hit by oncoming traffic. The headline screamed, *The Danger of the Downtown Look*, followed by text deriding the downtown boho style. Avery smirked, thinking of all the girls at Constance who tried to downgrade the simple elegance of their uniforms by pairing them with flip-flops, keffiyeh scarves, and ripped leggings. She was *definitely* going to like it here.

"This her?"

Avery glanced up. Standing at the glass door was a super-tall, super-skinny girl with a severe blond bob and whispery bangs framing her heart-shaped face. She was probably just out of college, and wore straight-leg jeans and a pink Thakoon blazer Avery had seen in this month's *Vogue*.

"Avery, this is McKenna Clarke," Goth Girl said as she turned back to her iMac.

"Avery Carlyle." Avery stood up and stuck her hand out formally. "So good to meet you, McKenna."

"Follow me." McKenna turned crisply on her four-inch purple suede Christian Louboutin ankle boots. Avery had to practically run to keep up with her as they walked down a white hallway.

"So, how long have you worked here?" Avery chirped, struggling to match McKenna's supermodel strut. Inside the office were rows and rows of cubicles. They passed a glass-walled conference room filled with willowy, pouty models. A harried-looking blond girl was frantically taking Polaroids of each of them.

McKenna sighed, not breaking her stride as she darted between racks of fur coats that had been set up, mazelike, in the hallway. "A year. And, listen, generally, interns are seen and not heard. That's just the way things are at *Metropolitan*."

Is it, now?

Finally, McKenna slowed down, in front of a glass-walled corner office. Avery could see Ticky, holding a rotary phone receiver in one hand and frantically typing on a typewriter with the other. Ticky's bright red henna-highlighted hair was teased a full three inches above her heavily Botoxed forehead, and she wore a beaded gold Chanel jacket.

"I'm going to just say hi to Ticky—she's expecting me," Avery explained, moving toward the '50s retro–style office.

"Shh!" McKenna hissed, wrapping her thin fingers around Avery's wrist and yanking her down the hall. She opened an unmarked door, pulled Avery in, and shut it behind her.

The room was a windowless space with shelves and shelves of beauty products. The ground was covered with containers of even more products. Three girls were sitting at one long desk, their shoulders hunched over laptops, and a phone kept ringing in the corner.

"Um, I think I'm supposed to talk to Ticky to see what she wants me to do. But thanks for your help," Avery said politely, moving again to the door.

McKenna shot Avery a death stare. "Listen, I'm in charge of all the interns, and I think it's best if you stay in the closet for a few days, until you learn more about the culture of *Metropolitan*. Gemma?" A brown-haired girl sitting at one of the computers turned around and raised her eyebrow.

"Come here, Intern," Gemma called impatiently, as she stood and walked toward a huge chest of plastic-laminate drawers. She pushed her black Prada frames further up on her ski-jump nose and looked Avery up and down.

Intern? She didn't even get called by *name*?

"So, I guess what I'll have you do is organize these drawers." Gemma turned to face Avery. She had a zit threatening to pop from her angular chin, and her complexion was splotchy, but she wore a Dries Van Noten gray sweaterdress over black leggings with zippers up the calves that accentuated her height. She looked cool, and she knew it.

Avery tried to smile through her disappointment. She quickly opened the drawer and began pulling out lipsticks, scattering them on a white counter that lined one wall. Okay, so this wasn't investigative reporting. Or photo-shoot styling. But it also wasn't hanging out with odd-smelling old ladies, which was all she'd done after school for the past few weeks.

Avery was in the middle of creating a drawer of light pink lip stains when the door creaked open again. McKenna.

"What's the burgundy doing here?" McKenna picked a MAC lip stain from the drawer of pale pinks and waved it accusingly in front of Avery's face.

Avery took it back guiltily, feeling like she was a kindergartener getting yelled at for not putting away her crayons properly. "Sorry," she muttered.

"You need to be more careful," Gemma warned, squinting down at the drawer.

"Anyway, since this is too complicated, there's a Stella sample sale down in the Meatpacking District. I wrote down a couple things. Would you mind fetching them for me? I'm a little smaller than you, so whatever's too tight on you will probably work." McKenna smiled angelically, passing Avery an AmEx.

Avery's eyes narrowed. Did McKenna want her to run out and do *her* personal shopping?

"Hope they take credit cards! Oh, also, since you're in the

nabe, can you return these to Jeffrey? These shoes totally aren't working for me. Or the magazine." McKenna arched her eyebrow.

Just then, Avery's cell phone rang loudly from her new Hermés purse: a Madonna-techno ringtone that Baby had set as her personal ring, just to be annoying.

"Is that a personal call?" McKenna was actually *tapping* her foot, as if she were a floor manager in a factory.

"Sorry." Avery furiously pushed silent on the phone, and instantly a text from her sister flashed: *Back from España!* Great. Her sister went to Spain, and all *she* got to do was go to the Meatpacking District.

Avery grabbed the heavy handles of McKenna's Jeffrey bag and turned crisply on her heel. She made her way out the of the office, marching past goth Angelina with her head held high. Her dream job might turn out to be a nightmare, but she wasn't about to break down for all of *Metropolitan* to see.

That's what the backseats of taxis are for.

the couch

Baby Carlyle's dirty white Havaiana flip-flops thwacked against the gleaming hardwood floors of Constance Billard on Friday afternoon. Officially, flip-flops weren't part of the uniform at the elite all-girls school, but Baby had broken so many rules lately that she doubted anyone would care. Her flight from Spain had landed just two hours ago, and all she wanted to do was crawl into bed and take a long nap. But as soon as she'd landed and turned her phone on, she'd received a frantic message from her mom saying that Mrs. McLean, Constance Billard's headmistress, wanted to see Baby *immediately*. Baby had known she'd have to face the headmistress eventually; after all, she'd skipped a week of school for her impromptu vacation.

Donna, the stringy-haired secretary, stuck her head out of the office as soon as Baby rounded the corner. "Mrs. McLean's waiting for you," she announced self-importantly.

"Thanks," Baby mumbled, shuffling into Mrs. McLean's inner office. It wasn't as if she needed directions. She'd already been here four times in the past month.

"Baby!" Mrs. McLean exclaimed, poking her large, doughy face around her office door.

Baby flashed her best *I'm just a dumb but endearing teenager who does impulsive things* smile. It was a look she'd mastered during her short time at Constance. She just hoped it'd be enough to persuade Mrs. McLean to let her behavior slide.

Again.

Baby plopped down in the center of the royal blue velvet love seat.

"Well, welcome back. Your mother called and told me to expect you today," Mrs. McLean began, sinking down behind her heavy oak desk. She normally favored bold-colored pantsuits from Talbots, but today, she wore a simple black jacket and skirt.

Baby nodded politely. More than anything, she wished she were back on La Rambla at an all-night café sipping a trifásico, the super-delicious alcohol-spiked coffee she'd discovered. A smile played on her lips as she remembered how one of the cute servers tried to teach her Catalan. It sounded so absurdly sexy, even if all he talked about was how much he loved his Vespa.

The whole experience had been magical. When she'd left, she was itching to just *go* somewhere, to get away from the status-obsessed world of the Upper East Side, where she still hadn't quite found her place.

"Baby, I'm concerned about you." Mrs. McLean leaned her fleshy forearms against the desk and peered at Baby thoughtfully. "Are *you* concerned about you?"

"I'm sorry," Baby said contritely. "I thought I'd be able to make everything up." She shrugged. Obviously, running off to Barcelona wasn't the most responsible thing to do, but she knew her classmates were taken out of school for weeks at a time for Gstaad skiing vacations or African safaris with their parents. It wasn't as if she'd missed anything important.

"It's not your grades," Mrs. McLean said ruefully, clearly wishing it *were* Baby's grades so she could hire a tutor and be done with it. "Frankly, it's your attitude. I've given you chances and we've tried some ways to make Constance more comfortable for you. Maybe it's time that you do the work and really prove to me that you want—and deserve—to be part of this community. You say you do, but your behavior says otherwise." Mrs. McLean pursed her lips together expectantly. "The only reason I'm letting you continue to stay is because of your involvement, however brief, with *Rancor*." She slid a thin magazine across the desk.

Baby peered at the cover, which said FOCUS ON FASHION in bubbly, pink scripted letters. Baby grinned. She and her class-mate Sydney Miller, a self-described womyn with a penchant for body piercings, had created a whole fashion spread with guys dressing in girls' clothes, and vice versa. It was cool and daring, and Baby was sad she hadn't been around when it came out.

"This caused quite a stir," Mrs. McLean said with a tight smile. "While I would have liked to discuss your, ahem, *artistic* vision, I do appreciate how hard you and Miss Miller worked on this."

"I can write a paper on the trip if that'd help." She focused on the spot between Mrs. McLean's bushy Bert and Ernie–style eye-brows. Teachers *loved* when kids offered to do extra work. Back in Nantucket, she'd written more than a few crappy extracurricular essays for her stoner boyfriend Tom so he wouldn't flunk out.

"No, that won't be necessary," Mrs. McLean replied dismis-sively. She began rifling through a huge Rolodex.

Baby's eyes narrowed. What could Mrs. McLean possibly have in mind? Scrubbing the Constance trophy case? Peeling wads of sugarless gum off the bottom of the birch-wood cafeteria tables?

"I'd like you to turn your taste for discovery *inward*," Mrs. McLean intoned. She yanked a card from the pile and slid it and a piece of paper across the desk. "I've already spoken with your mother about this. You are to complete twenty hours of therapy and have a therapist sign this form when your treatment is finished. I took the liberty of setting up your first appointment for this afternoon at four. That's in fifteen minutes," Mrs. McLean added in a warning tone.

"Thanks," Baby mumbled as she examined the thick ivory card suspiciously. DR. REBEKAH JANUS, PSYCHOTHERAPIST, was all it said, along with an address on Fifth Avenue. In a school surrounded by narcissistic, overdramatic, shopaholic girls, *she* was the one who needed therapy?

Mrs. McLean leaned forward on her elbows. "Dr. Janus is a therapist I recommend to many students, but if you have your own practitioner you'd rather use, that's fine. However, if you don't fulfill your twenty-hour therapy requirement by the end of the month, then you'll simply have to find a school that's a better fit."

Baby nodded. "I think you'll enjoy a journey of the mind." Mrs. McLean smiled as she walked Baby to the door.

"I guess," Baby agreed weakly. It wasn't like she had a choice.

Baby found her way to a brownstone on East Eightieth Street and walked into what seemed like a waiting room, decorated with tacky Van Gogh prints on the wall. Piles of back issues of *The New Yorker* and *The Economist* sat on an antique oak coffee table. Immediately, a door flung open.

"You're late," an immaculately dressed tall blond woman said smoothly.

"Sorry." Baby shrugged and shifted from one dirty flip-flopped foot to the other.

"Oftentimes a patient's punctuality says something about their feelings toward the process," the woman noted, as if she'd read Baby's mind. "I'm Dr. Janus." She stuck out her hand and Baby took it cautiously.

"Follow me," Dr. Janus said as she ushered Baby into her office. The walls and ceiling were bare and white, but the huge bay windows facing west lent a cheery glow to the otherwise stark room. "Now, lie down," Dr. Janus commanded, pointing at the low-slung leather couch in the center of the room. She sounded like she was trying to teach a dog a new trick.

Stay, Baby. Stay!

"I'll just sit." Baby spread the fabric of the gauzy maroon dress she'd bought from a street cart in Barcelona over her jeans.

"Lie down," Dr. Janus urged. "It's better that way."

Not wanting to seem rude, Baby flipped over on the couch and lay on her back, pulling up her knees. A collection of carved-wood elephant sculptures were clustered on a shelf, next to row after row of books by and about Freud. She wondered what the elephants were supposed to make her think of.

"Now, tell me about yourself," Dr. Janus said, her voice dropping an octave.

Baby stared up at the ceiling. "I'm Baby Carlyle. I'm sixteen and a triplet. I have a brother, Owen, and a sister, Avery, and we used to live in Nantucket. We moved to New York a month ago. And I just got in three hours ago from a trip to Barcelona and I am very tired," Baby added. Maybe Dr. Janus would take pity on her, fill out her form, and let her go home and take a nap.

"And?" Dr. Janus prompted from her desk. Baby turned and propped her head on her hand. What else was there? Baby turned back to Dr. Janus, hoping she'd ask another, less difficult question, sort of like how in French class Madame Rogers always switched to English as soon as she realized no one had any idea what the fuck she'd said.

"Don't look at me," Dr. Janus warned.

Baby sighed and flopped back on the couch. There was an ugly tan watermark staining the all-white ceiling. Was it some type of Rorschach test?

"What about your parents? Mom? Dad?" Dr. Janus prompted.

"I live with my mom. She's great. We don't know our dad. We were a surprise, probably courtesy of Burning Man." Before they were born Edie was a groupie who traveled around the country in the back of band buses. Avery was mortified by that part of their history, but Baby thought it was kind of cool.

"And?" Dr. Janus pressed.

"That's it," Baby said firmly. She didn't want to be one of those people who bitched about their parents ruining their lives. Sure, their mom was nutty, but she was also pretty fun.

"Fine." Dr. Janus sounded disappointed. "Tell me about Barcelona," she finally said.

"Barcelona was good," Baby replied, remembering. It *had* been good, but it had also felt like something was missing. She absentmindedly pulled her hair toward her mouth, chewing the ends. She used to do it just to gross Avery out when they were younger, but it was comforting and had become a habit.

"I just thought that getting out of New York would be good for me. You know, to get away from my family, away from school uniforms. Maybe I should become a nudist or something," Baby said randomly. She glanced up to see if Dr. Janus would crack a smile, but she just nodded blankly, as if Baby was actually intending to strip down. Baby self-consciously pulled her Nantucket High sweatshirt closer across her body. "Just kidding," she added lamely. What did Dr. Janus want from her anyway?

Besides $250 an hour?

"What were you looking for?" Dr. Janus prompted thoughtfully. A white noise machine in the background reminded Baby of the sound before a summer storm.

Baby crossed, then uncrossed her arms. This was all so contrived and designed to *be* relaxing that it had the opposite effect.

"Well, I was looking for Mateo. He was just this friend I met here in the city," she began. He'd told her that he'd come to New York on a dare with his best friend. It had seemed so unique and spontaneous that Baby had wanted to do the same sort of thing.

She knit her fingers together and held her hands above her head in a stretch. Maybe if she could just explain the situation rationally, Dr. Janus would understand how normal she was and that she didn't need twenty hours of mandatory therapy. "I thought he and I would just have fun. But then I couldn't find him, but I had a good time on my own. I mean, really, I just wanted to explore a new place—"

"Right, but what were you *looking* for?" Dr. Janus asked again, as if she were stuck on an endless repeat loop.

"Maybe an adventure, I guess. I mean, I just thought it'd

be fun." Baby frowned. That sounded kind of lame. "I mean, I thought it'd be a good way to find myself." There. That sounded more therapy-appropriate.

"I have a different theory," Dr. Janus said, her voice rising an octave in excitement. "What if I told you that you were looking for your father?"

Baby blinked. *Excuse me?* Sometimes Baby flipped through Edie's old bootleg tapes, trying to figure out if any songs were about her mother, in case her dad was some super-famous hippie rocker. But other than that, she rarely thought about it.

"No. I was looking for Mateo," Baby said firmly. She sat up, swinging her legs down off the couch. Weren't therapists supposed to let you come up with your *own* answers?

Dr. Janus sighed heavily. As if on cue, the white noise machine changed from the ocean sound track to a rainstorm one. A clap of fake thunder sounded. "It seems like you're spending more time hunting down boys than you are trying to discover yourself. What would you say to that?" Dr. Janus had her pen poised as though she were a court reporter.

Baby sighed in frustration.

"You're resistant," Dr. Janus said smoothly. "That's okay. This is a safe space. You don't have to talk. You can lie there until the hour is up," she offered, examining her nude-polished fingernails.

"Isn't that kind of pointless?" Baby asked rudely. If she was just going to lie around, she'd much rather do it in her own bed, thank you very much.

"It's not pointless at all." Dr. Janus opened her eyes even wider, and Baby realized she was a little cross-eyed. One blue eye remained fixed on Baby while the other one looked down at her paper. It was extremely disconcerting. "What you need is to learn your inner motivations. And it's going to take a while," she explained matter-of-factly. "You'll probably want to come in every day," she concluded as she closed her small leather-bound notebook.

"What?" Baby flung up suspiciously. What could she *possibly* talk about every day?

"We're going to go on a journey into your psyche together." Dr. Janus clapped her hands together in rapture, as if she couldn't wait. "Who knows? One of my patients has been with me for the past twenty years. You wouldn't believe the work we've done together." She nodded importantly.

"Can I think about this and call you?" Baby asked. Not waiting for an answer, she stood up, then bolted toward the door and slammed it shut.

"You didn't *really* close the door to personal enlightenment, you know," Dr. Janus yelled from the other side. Baby hurriedly opened the door to the hallway, ignoring the doorman as she burst outside.

Freedom!

rien de rien

"I need a Brazilian—anyone want to come with me?" Sarah Jane Jenson asked as she, Jiffy Bennett, Genevieve Coursy, and Jack Laurent walked out the doors of Constance Billard. They rushed past the windows to get out of sight of the headmistress's office.

Jack fought the urge to roll her eyes. Why would Sarah Jane Jenson, who hadn't had a boyfriend since camp in eighth grade, and wasn't planning on going to the beach anytime soon, *possibly* need a Brazilian bikini wax? Several tenth graders clustered on Constance's front steps immediately glanced over, eager to hear Jack's response.

"I wish I could," Jack lied. She dug into her voluminous blue Balenciaga city bag, fishing out a pack of Merits. She lit up and then passed the pack to Genevieve, keeping an eye out for her boyfriend, J.P. Cashman. He didn't like that she smoked, and after their brief breakup just a few weeks ago, she didn't want to rock the boat. "I'm hanging out with J.P. this afternoon."

"But it'd be like a present to him!" Jiffy justified. Jiffy had never really had a boyfriend, but her thirty-two-year-old socialite sister

Beatrice had already been married three times, so she considered herself an expert on guys.

"That's such a male-centric view," Genevieve said dismissively, exhaling smoke in Jiffy's face. She'd recently started reading Simone de Beauvoir in an attempt to be cast in her director dad's new Sartre biopic, and it was really rubbing off on her. Pretty soon she'd get her nipples pierced and start hanging out with that weird possible lesbian Sydney. Jack wrinkled her nose. She was *so* glad she had a boyfriend.

"What's *wrong* with being male-centric?" Jiffy countered, brushing her way-too-long wispy brown bangs out of her brown eyes. She turned to Jack. "Please come? We've hardly *seen* you since you got back together with J.P.!" she pleaded.

"I can't. Besides, waxing isn't exactly a group activity," Jack responded boredly, even though a quick appointment—by *herself*—at the Elizabeth Arden Red Door salon on Fifth might not be such a bad idea. Things with J.P. *had* been going especially well lately. Maybe it was time they finally did it. *It* it. Jack turned sharply on her heel and walked toward Fifth Avenue. Immediately, just like she knew they would, the other girls followed.

"Um, the problem with being male-centric is that guys don't like that. Guys like it when girls don't give a fuck," Genevieve explained in exasperation, exhaling another cloud of smoke. Sarah Jane nodded thoughtfully.

"Baby Carlyle doesn't give a fuck," Jiffy mused as she practically jogged to keep up with Jack's long strides

Jack whirled around and glared at her. Could Jiffy really be dense enough to bring up Baby fucking Carlyle in front of her? Baby had briefly dated J.P., and the last Jack heard, she'd run off to Spain or Switzerland or something. And that was fine by her.

"Sorry, Jack!" Jiffy exclaimed, seeing the look on Jack's face. "But I wonder where she is. I mean, who just disappears?"

"I heard she was getting a sex change." Genevieve shrugged. "Whatever, why does she matter? The point is that Jack and J.P. are together."

Jack smiled at Genevieve, glad that someone was making sense. The girls kept talking, but Jack tuned them out as she walked a few steps ahead. She had much better things to think about than Baby Carlyle—such as tomorrow's itinerary. She'd head over to Elizabeth Arden during double photography, then go home with J.P. after school and casually lie on his bed and . . .

"Hey ladies!" J.P. called from the opposite side of the street, interrupting Jack's little X-rated fantasy. Jack threw her Merit down, dangerously close to Genevieve's black Tory Burch flats. She fluttered her Dior Black Out mascaraed eyelashes at him in an *I'm innocent* gesture.

"Hey handsome!" Jack threw her arms around him as soon as he crossed, mostly for the viewing pleasure of her friends. He was wearing a perfectly pressed blue oxford shirt and an unfortunate Riverside Prep baseball cap that did *nothing* for his brown hair.

"This is for you, princess." J.P. grinned as he handed Jack a steaming venti Starbucks cup. "Do you girls need anything?" He cracked his perfect smile and Sarah Jane and Jiffy giggled. Jack resisted the urge to kick their Wolford stocking–clad shins.

J.P. was the son of Dick Cashman, a major real estate mogul, but he wasn't an asshole about it. He was generous, funny, and smart, and they'd been dating for just about *forever*. Except, of course, for when he'd broken up with Jack just a few weeks earlier for Baby, a brilliant match that had lasted all of a week. As a method of psychological warfare, Jack had pretended to date

Baby's brother, Owen, only to walk in on *him* hooking up with some slutty Seaton Arms girl. Now, Jack and J.P. were back together, and Baby was God knew where, becoming a man or whatever, and everyone was happy.

Another Upper East Side fairy tale.

"See you girls later," Jack called, hurriedly steering J.P. down the street. The girls looked disappointed to see them go. Too bad. Maybe they could get their *own* boyfriends.

Jack concentrated on the feeling of J.P.'s hand firmly guiding the curve of her back as they walked west, toward Central Park. The leaves were falling off the few lonely trees, and the sky was cloudy, but she loved days like these. They felt so European, the perfect backdrop for a love affair. She took a large sip of the latte, feeling the warm liquid travel down her throat. It felt so *good* to be with someone who remembered that she needed two Splendas to make it sweet.

"I missed you," J.P. said, giving Jack's arm a squeeze. Her stomach fluttered. She wanted to scream to everyone walking down the street, from the nanny with two kids in a stroller to the old man in an elegant Oscar de la Renta suit navigating the sidewalk with his cane, that this was her *boyfriend*.

Jack's life had been a shitstorm this past month: Her banker father had cut her and her mother off, forcing them to move out of their luxurious town house and into its attic, and refused to pay for anything except school. But things were starting to look up. First, her father had relented over dinner at Le Cirque last week and given her a monthly, prepaid debit card. It was the personal finance program he had in place for Jack's kindergarten-age stepsisters, but it was nice not to be scrounging for quarters to buy Diet Cokes from the vending machine. She'd also nailed two scholarship auditions for her ballet program and was just waiting for a call to let her know she'd been accepted into the School of American Ballet's prestigious apprenticeship program. And, most importantly, she and J.P. were back together.

"You look good," Jack said as she reached up and pulled his tacky Riverside Prep cap off his head. She stuffed it in her purse. *There*. Now he looked even better.

"Want to go over to my place?" J.P. asked as they approached the gigantic interlocking-C sculptures that marked the Cashman Complexes, one of the many buildings owned by J.P.'s father. He lived in the penthouse with his dad and his European former–fashion model mother.

"Not today." Jack smiled mysteriously. She actually did have other plans. Even though she was *almost* positive she'd gotten the dance scholarship, she hadn't gotten a definite yes. That meant she had to take pay-as-you-go classes at Steps, a studio on the Upper West Side, which was above a Fairway supermarket and always smelled like bacon. Besides, even though she loved being back with J.P., she still wasn't 100 percent sure she could count on him not to ditch her again. With her luck, Baby Carlyle would probably come *back* a man and J.P. would decide he was gay.

He *does* dress well. . . .

"Okay." J.P. nodded agreeably. "I'll call you?" He pulled her face toward his and kissed her. His mouth tasted familiar and reassuring, like eucalyptus mixed with spearmint gum. "See you later, babe," he called, waving as he whooshed through the gold revolving door of his building.

"Bye," Jack called, as if to herself. She suddenly shivered, pulling her Marc by Marc Jacobs leather bomber jacket closer around her shoulders. The jacket had been a total mistake, bought on clearance at one of those tacky designers-for-less websites—just one more reminder that things *had* changed since the last time she and J.P. had been dating.

She continued to walk down Fifth, pausing when she came to Seventy-second Street, the street the Carlyles lived on. She looked up toward the top floor, but all the windows were dark and it was impossible to see anything from the street. Not like she was looking for something. After all, she and Owen hadn't *really* been dating at all.

Finally, she made her way to her town house (she still thought of it as hers, even though another family lived downstairs) on Sixty-third between Fifth and Madison, where she'd change before heading to Steps. She snuck in the back entrance and lightly walked up the stairs to the attic, hoping her overly dramatic, French former-ballerina mother wouldn't be home.

"Ah, cherie!" Jack's mother flew out of her bedroom and into their cramped foyer, knocking over a rickety hat stand in excitement. Her red hair stood askew around her face like an unchecked campfire.

"Hi Mom." Jack's mood darkened. Her mother wore a flowy, muumuu-style Diane von Furstenberg sample sale error over her thin ex-dancer frame. She still had a certain elegance about her, though, and looked a little bit like Norma Desmond, the crazy aging actress from the movie *Sunset Boulevard*.

"Today Paris, tomorrow the world!" Vivienne Restoin cried. "I will be drinking real Sancerre by sunset." One Gitane cigarette hung limply between her mother's fingers. Someday she'd seriously burn down the house in a dramatic fit.

Maybe then they could move somewhere nicer.

"Okay, well, have a good trip." Jack shrugged. This was news?

Vivienne always went to Paris to see her old ballerina friends and gossip about the old days, when they'd all dated much wealthier, much older men. That was how Vivienne and Jack's dad had met.

Jack brushed past her mother and dropped her purse on top of the ugly spinach-green couch in the living room. The garret was furnished with Vivienne's most egregious decorator mistakes, making the entire apartment look like the showroom for the Housing Works thrift shop.

"'Have a good trip'! My comedienne!" Vivienne exclaimed affectionately, trailing behind Jack. "*We* are leaving. I received the call about my show. You call your father—*le bâtard*—and have him make arrangements for your schooling," Vivienne commanded, her cigarette flying through the air.

Jack paused. A week ago, Vivienne had vaguely mentioned a possible part in some French soap opera, but Jack had assumed she'd confused it with some weird dream she'd had or play she'd seen. But now her mom sounded 100 percent sure of herself. What the fuck? Did that mean she was expected to move to Paris while her mom played out her totally lame comeback on French television?

"I'm not going," Jack stated flatly.

"But you must. You and me, we are a team. You cannot desert me now. And this is just the beginning for us," Vivienne went on, her eyes gleaming. She tottered over to the mantel and picked up a silver Tiffany frame that contained a picture of herself as a prima ballerina at the Paris Opera House. Jack wanted to grab the frame, throw it on the floor, and stamp on it. Could her mom be a *little* less self-obsessed and realize for just a second that she was *ruining* her only daughter's life?

"How could you do this to me? What about me?" Jack fought to keep her voice steady. She sounded like a third-rate actress in a crappy reality TV drama. At this rate, they'd sign her up to costar with her mom on whatever the fuck the show was called.

Le Insane?

"*La folie des jeunes,*" Vivienne said disdainfully, artfully flinging her hand so the ash from her still-burning cigarette fluttered to the scuffed wooden floorboards. She came over and wrapped her skinny arms around Jack. Jack stood ramrod straight, refusing to hug her mother and let her think for a *moment* she approved of this. "Your life hasn't begun yet, darling," Vivienne cooed into her ear.

"We leave on Sunday. *Nous devons preparer!*" As if to emphasize her point, Vivienne flung open the hall closet, pulled out a chinchilla coat, and wrapped it around her skinny body.

Jack stomped into her bedroom and slammed the door. Angry tears slipped down her face. She wiped them away with the back of her hand. She picked up her Treo and dialed 1 for J.P.

"I'm coming over," Jack announced flatly. There was no way she could concentrate on a dance class this afternoon. She needed a different type of physical activity to distract her from what was going on. She opened her closet and shoved her favorite pair of skinny Citizens and a gray Theory sweater into her purse. Then she opened her bureau drawer and pulled out a pair of pink Cosabella panties she'd bought last spring at Barneys and a lacy black La Perla bra. She frowned. Was the color combination too do-me? She always bought sexy underwear, but so far, she'd never taken it off for J.P.

There's a first time for everything. . . .

The strains of "Non, Je Ne Regrette Rien," her mother's favorite Edith Piaf song, emanated from beyond the door. Usually, Vivienne would only listen to it after drinking an entire bottle of wine. Jack wanted no part in that. She didn't have time to think—she needed to get *out*. She shoved the lingerie into her purse, raced out of her room, and clattered down the stairs, not bothering to say goodbye. Maybe her mom would think she'd run away. Then she'd be sorry.

She hurried uptown in the growing darkness, trying to imagine Paris. She'd lived there over the summer, as a dance student at the Paris Opera House. Yes, it was beautiful, but it wasn't *New York*. She pulled her pack of Merits from her bag and furiously clicked her Tiffany lighter. This was an emergency. Besides, why quit now? Everyone fucking smoked in France.

See, there's always a silver—make that smoke-filled—lining.

there's more than one way to spell heartbreak

Rhys Sterling walked onto the deck of the pool of the Ninety-second Street Y in a daze, still wearing his St. Jude's school uniform, complete with blazer. He didn't want to go into the locker room and risk running into Owen. He could easily break down at any moment. Just being around people was too much work. All he wanted to do was lie in a dark room until college.

He squinted in the bright fluorescent lights of the pool. The JV and varsity swimmers were all on the pool deck, huddled tightly around Coach Siegel, their eyes wide with fear. Coach Siegel had been a champion swimmer and partier at Stanford, and loved giving his swimmers advice on girls outside of practice. But during practice, and especially during meets, Coach was super tough. And right now, he didn't look happy. His chiseled young face was bright red and his jaw was clenched. Cautiously, Rhys edged over to the team.

"Sterling, buddy, there's a problem!" Coach Siegel yelled as soon as he noticed Rhys. He took a Speedo from the large cardboard box by his feet and threw it over. Rhys halfheartedly reached up to grab it, but he missed and it fluttered to the wet pool deck. He glanced down. He could clearly make out the scripted, embroidered words on the material: ST. DUDES.

Rhys racked his brain. It was a miracle he'd even remembered to send in the swimsuit orders from the sports shop at all last week, since it was right after he'd caught Kelsey and Owen together. And maybe he'd been upset and distracted, but St. *Dudes*? Wouldn't the operator or the manufacturer or hell, even the *embroiderer* realize how absurd that was? Rhys shook his head in disbelief, holding his palms over his eyes. Maybe when he looked again, everything would be back to normal.

"I'm sorry, Coach," he said finally, not sure what else to say.

Coach nodded slowly. "Well, there's nothing we can do now. Guys, get in and warm up. Try to stay underwater so no one reads your suits. Sterling, let's have a little discussion." The guys began grumbling, but broke off and headed toward the starting blocks. Coach motioned for Rhys to follow him.

Coach led him to an empty section of blue metal bleachers in the corner. Rhys sat down with a thud. "Sterling, buddy, you've got to step it up!" Coach stared down at him with his intense blue eyes. Rhys's ears felt like they were filled with water. This was going to be the *you suck and you're supposed to be a leader* speech. And the truth was, he sort of did suck. He couldn't even order fucking *swimsuits* right.

"I'll get new suits, Coach. Sorry," Rhys said woodenly, staring straight ahead. He tried not to notice Owen dive into the pool. Despite the fact he was late to the warm-up, he was easily cutting through the water, looking as sharp as ever. Rhys placed his hands over his eyes.

"My man, forget about the suits for a second." Coach slid

onto the bleacher next to him and awkwardly patted his shoulder. "I know you got dumped. I hear things. You may not believe it, but it's even happened to me." Coach chuckled. Rhys nodded, trying not to look away from the floor. Like knowing Coach had been dumped was supposed to make him feel better about the fact that his whole fucking life sucked?

"But you've gotta carry on!" Coach pounded his fist into his hand rigorously, gaining steam. "You're the captain. And when you're hurting, the team's hurting. And that hurts me." His reddish-brown eyebrows furrowed in concern. "I don't care what you guys do, but it's up to you to get it together. You're my captain. Now, is there anything you want to tell me?"

"It's . . . complicated," Rhys finally muttered. If he even said Kelsey's name, he'd cry. And if he said Owen's name, he'd . . .

Cry some more?

"Love is complicated!" Coach boomed. "Let's figure this out. I can't have you thinking about this in the pool—it'll just slow you down. I remember, back in my sophomore year there was this smokin' volleyball player. Her name was Sunny, she was a junior, and her rack was—"

"Uh, sir?" Rhys asked, glancing at the scratched-up gold Rolex on Coach's wrist. The swim meet was supposed to start in five minutes. "Should I make sure everyone's ready?"

"What?" Coach stood up, pulled out of his reverie. "Yes. And you know what? I'm glad we had this conversation. Girls pull off your balls." Coach stroked his chin thoughtfully. "Emotionally speaking," he added.

Rhys nodded numbly, playing with the zipper on his swim bag.

"Okay, go warm up. We've got to keep our focus, Sterling." Coach clapped him on the back in a manly way. "It's going to be a tight one, and I'm counting on you and Carlyle to go one-two in the hundred free. Got it?"

Suddenly, the white shorts–clad official on the pool deck blew his whistle, signaling the end of the warm-up period. Rhys headed to the locker room to change. He wasn't sure if he even had the energy to swim today.

"Dude, what the fuck?" Ken Williams roughly pushed Rhys as he passed by. Ken looked more like a linebacker than a long-distance swimmer, and it wasn't a secret that his parents still sent him to fat camp every summer. His pasty body was squeezed into his Speedo. It was *not* an attractive look. "St. fucking Dudes? We look like tools. I'm never going to get ladies this way!"

"Sorry, man." Rhys didn't bother to stop walking. His mind kept flashing back to an image of Kelsey and Owen in front of the Y. They'd been all over each other. And if they were *that* close in public, he couldn't imagine what they were doing in private. . . .

Actually, he could. And it was more than he and Kelsey had ever done in three years of going out.

By the time Rhys collected himself in the bathroom stall, changed, and walked back on deck, the meet was already well under way. The bleachers were peppered with fans of the Orioles, who came from some private school on Long Island.

"Sterling!" Coach grabbed his shoulder from behind. "We're down, you and Carlyle are up for your race *now*, and you're beating off in the locker room. Just get in," he spat, their earlier heart-to-heart clearly forgotten.

Rhys stepped on the block for the hundred freestyle, his best event. He saw Owen swinging his arms back and forth easily, loosening up.

"Swimmers, take your mark," the official in the corner intoned, and Rhys leaned down over the water. The start machine beeped, and he dove in. As soon as Rhys surfaced, he knew everything was wrong. He began pulling the water with his arms, but they felt like lead, and all he could see was Owen ahead of him. As Rhys slogged through the water, he realized it was fucking pointless. By the flip turn, it was obvious that Owen was going to win. Just like he'd gotten Kelsey. Just like he'd taken over Rhys's whole goddamn life.

Rhys glided to the finish, seeing the Orioles slam one by one into the wall as he leisurely slid into last place. One of them leaned over the lane line to shake his hand, but Rhys shook his head and pulled himself out of the water. He walked over to the stands, picked up his swim bag, and flung it over his shoulder, ignoring the St. Jude's guys who gathered around him. He saw Coach's face turn tomato-red in anger in the stands, but he didn't care.

"Duuuudes!" The Oriole team began chanting maniacally from the stands. "*You're awesome, St. Dudes!!!*" Rhys squinted down at the still blue water in the pool. It reminded him of Kelsey's eyes. He couldn't be here anymore.

Coach ran up to him. "Sterling, what the fuck was that?"

"I quit," he said. His voice cracked as it echoed off the concrete walls of the pool, and he realized everyone was staring at him. He didn't even care. Being in the same room with Carlyle was just too fucking much. His chest felt tight and rage coursed through his veins. He walked off the pool deck and into the locker room, his flip-flops squelching against the wet floor. The other team was still jeering.

"Guys. Meeting. My office. Now!" Coach bellowed, his voice echoing off the tiled, windowless walls.

"Coach?" Owen was standing to the left of him, still dripping from the race. Someone had to do *something*. Owen felt a shiver run down his back. It was his fault that Rhys had had his meltdown in the first place.

"Everyone in my office, now," Coach repeated in a low growl. One by one, the guys huddled in the tiny, damp-floored multipurpose office in the back of the locker room. No one seemed to know what was happening, or if anyone should go out and look for Rhys. Owen glanced around at the uncertain expressions of his teammates, but no one would catch his eye. He crossed his arms over his chest and looked down at the floor.

Coach burst in and slammed the door shut. The room suddenly felt a hundred degrees hotter. "This is not the team I signed up to coach. If I wanted drama, I'd become a fucking theater teacher." He slammed his hand against the cracked plastic laminated desk and began to pace, his Adidas slides making suctioning sounds as he weaved around the team. "Do any of you know what the fuck is going on with Rhys?" Coach looked at each member of the team. Owen held his breath. Would one of the guys explain the full story of why Rhys quit? If Coach knew that he stole Kelsey . . . Owen sighed heavily.

"Carlyle?" Coach barked, his eyes resting directly on him. Owen felt a blush rise up his chest.

"No, Coach. But don't worry, we'll pick it up," he said. What else was he supposed to say?

"You guys better," Coach said, stomping toward the door. "Carlyle's our new captain. Better rest up, because next week will be hell." He stormed out of the office, then popped his head back in. "You guys can lose the rest of the meet by yourselves. I'm not going to watch. Just fix the fucking suits before I see you again."

Owen stared at his teammates. They were all still in a state of shock; Chadwick and Ian's eyes were wide and terrified. Owen stood and moved toward the door. None of the guys followed him. "Guys?" he asked, his voice wavering and uncertain. Chadwick set his wide-eyed, terrified gaze on Hugh.

"Get back out there, you homos. Let's finish the meet!" Hugh yelled, sounding much more sure of himself than Owen did. He took one of Coach's orange whistles from a pencil cup on the desk and blew it loudly. One by one the guys began to slowly stand.

"That's more like it!" Owen cheered as they shuffled back onto the pool deck. See? They just needed to regroup, and they'd be *fine*. "Let's get back out there!"

Aye-aye, Captain!

o makes a uniform decision

From: Owen.Carlyle@StJudes.edu
To: SwimTeam_All@StJudes.edu
Date: Friday, October 15, 6:00pm
Subject: St. Dudes

Hey guys,
I put in a rush order for new suits—and double-checked the spelling! I'm picking them up on Sunday at Paragon Sports on Eighteenth at five. Let's make it an official swim team outing and then have a "conditioning" practice with brews? We need to put the loss to Oriole behind us and focus on the season ahead.
Peace,
Owen

as long as they have each other . . .

"My life sucks," Avery announced loudly on Friday evening as she stomped into the Carlyles' penthouse apartment. She slammed the door and threw her beige Miu Miu trench on the blue velvet wingback chair in the foyer that basically acted as an overpriced coat hanger.

"Hello?" Avery called again when no one answered. Someone better be home. All she wanted to do was order pizza, eat as much fattening food as possible, and forget about *Metropolitan* and lip glosses and bitchy assistants for the weekend.

"Hi!" Baby popped her head up from the gunmetal gray Jonathan Adler couch in the center of the gigantic living room. "Join the club—my life sucks too," she called.

"What's your problem? You just got back from *vacation*." Avery eyed her tiny sister critically and stomped over to the couch. Baby's hair was haphazardly piled on top of her head in sort of an Amy Winehouse–style beehive, and she wore baggy shorts and an oversize T-shirt, but somehow she looked like a supermodel instead of a drug-addled mess.

She was surrounded by the small, leather-bound photo albums

they'd brought from Nantucket. Avery grabbed one of the albums lying by Baby's feet and quickly paged through it. It was from the summer between eighth and ninth grade, when they'd spent every afternoon on the beach. In all of the photos, Baby was smiling, usually with several guys looking on. Avery picked up another album, this time of the triplets when they were toddlers. Even a picture of them when they were just three showed Baby running out of the frame. Typical. Avery was obsessively into creating lists and plans, while Baby just sort of floated through life.

"Mrs. McLean isn't too happy with me." Baby smiled ruefully. "I have to go to twenty hours of therapy. She's making me." Baby shrugged. "My first session was today."

Avery plopped on the couch, causing their cat, Rothko, to meow loudly and run away. Was she supposed to feel *sorry* for Baby? Because she didn't. In fact, she felt totally exasperated by her. Of *course* her sister could ditch school for a week and just get a slap on the wrist and mandatory therapy.

"What'd the therapist say?" Avery finally probed, her curiosity getting the better of her.

"I'm apparently overdependent on men and haven't fully completed the detachment process from our dad, whoever he is." Baby rolled her dark brown eyes and lay back on the couch, staring up at the ceiling. Wasn't therapy supposed to make you feel *better* about yourself?

"Oh," Avery said blankly. "How are you going to fix that?"

"I have no idea." Baby tried to force herself to smile. She picked up another photo album, desperate to find some type of clue into her inner psyche. So far, she had nothing. Maybe that was her problem: She never *thought* about what she was doing, whether it was running back to Nantucket or flying to Barcelona, she just . . . did it. And usually there was a guy involved. Was Dr. Janus right? Was she using boys to hide from herself? She shoved the photo album and it fell to the floor with a clatter.

"Hellooooo?" The thin, singsongy voice of their mother, Edie Carlyle, called out from the foyer. Edie was in her mid-forties, and if not for the laugh lines etched on her tanned face, could have passed for the triplets' older sister. She had dark blond bobbed hair currently pulled into tiny twists, and wore a bright pink hand-dyed peasant skirt with a furry brown sweater that looked like it was made from gorilla hair. "Oh good, you're here!" She clapped her hands together excitedly.

Yippee!

"I'm going on a date with Remington. Of course, I told you about him."

Avery and Baby looked at each other. Back in Nantucket, their mother had never dated, preferring to be wholly engaged in her *art*—which could either refer to her children or her weird 3-D chicken-wire sculptures in their backyard.

Seeing the confused looks on her daughters' faces, Edie went on. "Don't you remember, darlings? My high school sweetheart? Oh, it was just so wonderful! Absolutely out of *nowhere* he showed up at the collaborative in Red Hook last week, and I could not believe my eyes. He looks very different now, of course, but just as handsome as ever. . . ." Edie's blue eyes glazed over at the memory of her high school love. "I was an artist, he was destined for business school, and in the end we went our separate ways. He worked in finance for years and years, but now he invests in the art world, which is how we ended up in the same place! Can you *imagine*?"

Avery stared at her mother blankly. She really couldn't.

"We're going to walk to Brooklyn! How do I look?" Edie twirled again and glanced expectantly at her daughters.

"You look really *colorful*," Avery finally mustered, grinning impishly at Baby. Actually, her mom looked great. She couldn't remember the last time she'd seen her so . . . glowy.

"Oh, you girls are impossible." Edie's sterling silver turtle-shaped earrings swung wildly back and forth. "I think I look fabulous," she crowed as she floated off. "Don't wait up!" she called as the front door of the penthouse slammed behind her.

"Move over." Avery rolled off the arm of the couch and onto the cushion. How was it that her *mom* had a date and she didn't? She was a dateless, errand-running *nobody*. "Did you know they're calling me 'the intern' at work?" Avery asked, feeling extremely sorry for herself. She poked her sister's arm to make sure she was listening. If Avery wanted to have a pity party, Baby had better be a good guest.

"Well, aren't you the intern?" Baby shrugged.

"Whatever." Avery sighed. The rest of the school year stretched ahead of her in week after week of thankless labor. She felt like a pre-ball Cinderella, with no Prince Charming in sight.

"Want to make cookies?" Baby asked unexpectedly, swinging her legs off the couch and wandering toward the kitchen. Avery stomped after her. Cookies would *not* make everything better.

Unless they're the jumbo chocolate chocolate-chip cookies from City Bakery, that is.

Baby began flinging open cabinets and throwing the mismatched packages of spelt, granola, and brown sugar that Edie picked up at her favorite Park Slope co-op onto the counter. Edie didn't trust any of the small gourmet grocery shops dotting Madison Avenue. Avery frowned as she examined the ingredients strewn across the large, stainless steel kitchen island in the center of the room.

"Let's call this *cooking our demons*." Baby winked, imitating their mom's ridiculous white magic incantations. Avery smiled in spite of herself. Baby was irresponsible and maddening, but she was also her sister and would do anything to try to cheer her up. Avery picked up a half-open brown bag of flaxseed and dumped it in the trash.

"I need chocolate," she announced. She climbed onto the granite countertop and opened one of the top cabinets, tossing a package of chocolate chips down to Baby.

As the two girls set to work, Avery smiled to herself. Maybe her life didn't suck so bad. Really, what was so bad about spending a Friday night baking cookies?

Um, besides *everything*?

An hour later, the kitchen was filled with the aroma of baking cookies and Avery and Baby were sitting next to each other on the black granite counter, kicking their legs back and forth against the cabinets below as they companionably drank from a bottle of organic red wine that had been sitting on the counter forever. Avery took a large swig, swishing the liquid around her mouth thoughtfully. Back in Nantucket, she'd always imagined she'd be sipping champagne at fabulous New York City parties, not sipping homemade wine at *home*. This internship was becoming one more disaster she could add to an already long list of Upper East Side errors. And she'd been in New York for less than two months.

"Don't be upset over the intern thing. It was only your first day," Baby said, as if reading her mind. "Besides, it's kind of cool that no one knows your real name. That way you can fly under the radar."

"Thanks," Avery said, meaning it. "You want real food?" she added. She hopped off the counter and began rifling through a basket full of menus, junk mail, and new-age hippie magazines that had recently come in the mail. Edie never opened the mail. Luckily, she had an accountant who handled all the bills, or else they'd be chased by debtors.

"I'll take that." Baby grabbed a magazine called *Inner Healing*. A picture of a heart that looked like it had been drawn by a four-year-old was on the cover.

"Why do you need that?" Avery asked suspiciously. "You already *have* a therapist." Avery pulled out the menu for John's Pizza and dialed the number. John's was a totally touristy destination in Times Square, but they had other outposts, and the one over on York and Sixty-third had the best brick-oven pizza ever.

"I don't think therapy will work for me," Baby confessed, after Avery had ordered. The back of the magazine was full of weird ads for alternative healers. *Color away your confusion with crayons!* No thank you. *Rebirth into the authentic you.* No. *Scream therapy.* Hah. *Find your inner ocean.* Baby paused at this one. *Are you looking to rediscover your natural self?* the text read. That didn't sound *too* dippy. And it was way better than Dr. Janus's freaky Oedipus complex fixation.

"What's that?" Avery asked nosily. Baby yanked the magazine away, suddenly shy. She didn't want to tell Avery that she was actually considering trying to find her inner ocean.

"Whatever." Avery lost interest as she opened the polished chrome door of the never-been-used-until-now oven.

"Are you making cookies?" Owen burst into the kitchen. Their brother had some kind of internal radar that always led him to food. "Yum!" He grabbed three and stuffed them in his mouth.

"Where's your girlfriend?" Baby asked as she tore the *find your ocean* page from the magazine, folded it, and stuffed it in the pocket of her baggy brown corduroy shorts.

"She had . . . a game." Owen paused. Was it field hockey? Tennis? He vaguely remembered Kelsey explaining to him why they couldn't meet tonight, but he couldn't remember what she'd said. Whenever they were together, he found it kind of hard to pay attention.

Wonder why?

"Maybe a tennis match." Owen shrugged and grabbed two more cookies. "Did you order food already?" he asked, flicking through the menus.

"Yeah, I got the pepperoni-sausage heart-attack special just for you," Avery teased. "But wait, didn't you have a meet today too?"

"Yeah." Owen nodded. "Actually, they made me captain." Saying it sounded pretty cool, even though they'd lost the meet.

"Oh my God," Avery squealed. "Congratulations!" She squeezed her brother's arm affectionately. "What did Kelsey say?"

"I didn't tell her yet," Owen said. In fact, it might be awkward letting her know, since he was basically replacing Rhys.

In more ways than one.

"What?" Avery demanded. The only thing she loved more than nosing into her sister's life was nosing into her brother's. "How have you not told her yet? What do you guys do together, anyway?"

Owen's ears turned bright red.

"Eew!" Avery squealed.

Owen grinned. He couldn't help it. Just thinking about Kelsey made him happy.

Or horny. Close enough.

"You need to go on a real date," Avery commanded, taking in her brother's gross horndog face. When was he going to learn that city girls were more sophisticated, more mature, more *everything* than girls in Nantucket?

More uptight?

She pulled out her pink Treo and expertly typed with a maroon-polished fingernail. Owen stuffed two more cookies in his mouth. A date might not be a bad idea.

"I'm making a reservation for you at One if by Land, Two if by Sea for tomorrow night. It's super romantic." Avery nodded authoritatively, as if the deal was settled. If he was going to hold on to Kelsey, he needed to treat her right. "Pick her up in a town car and don't forget to bring flowers."

Owen smiled as he hopped onto one of the steel bar stools surrounding the kitchen island. It was sweet of his sister to organize this, but it almost sounded like *she* was the one who needed the date. He was about to offer to set her up with one of the swim team guys when the buzzer rang, announcing their pizza delivery.

Saved by the bell.

who says j can't go home?

"Morning, gorgeous."

Jack felt a hand stroking her bare shoulder. She snapped awake, staring at the unfamiliar sea foam-green wall above her. Where the fuck was she?

She turned and saw J.P. standing above her, holding a gold *C*-emblazoned mug and wearing a cashmere bathrobe. "Coffee?" he asked.

"Thanks." Jack grabbed the cup, trying to remember how she'd gotten to J.P.'s. She was still wearing her jeans and paper-thin C&C California tank top from last night. Finally she remembered coming to his apartment, drinking six vodka sodas in quick succession while bitching to J.P. about her mom and Paris and her ridiculous acting revival, then falling asleep.

The hazelnut smell of the coffee suddenly made her feel extremely nauseated.

"You all right?" J.P. asked in concern. "My dad wants us to have breakfast with him and my mom. Is that okay?" he asked anxiously. Jack nodded, even though the thought of food made her feel more than a little sick.

"I just need to shower," she said, throwing an arm over her pounding head.

"Want company?" J.P. asked hopefully. When she'd left her apartment last night, it had seemed like a good idea for them to do it, but it felt sort of gross to lose her virginity on a night when she'd just found out she was either leaving the country or homeless. Instead, she'd gotten extremely drunk and passed out fully clothed.

Great solution.

When Jack didn't answer, he just shifted on the edge of the bed and stroked her long red hair. It was a little weird to be together in the morning, with him barefoot and wearing a robe. She'd slept over before, but only when his parents were out of town and the rest of their friends were also passed out on every available bed and couch.

"I need a shower." Jack pulled away. She needed a lot of things: a not-crazy family, a place to live, a deep-tissue massage. But for now, a shower would do.

Finally, Jack was clean and feeling slightly less disgusting, even though the only underwear she'd had to change into was the extremely sexy set she'd planned to wear last night. She examined herself critically in the bathroom mirror. Had all the stress made her skinnier? Her face looked angular, and now that her blond highlights had grown out into a much more natural russet color, she looked older and more sophisticated. She pulled her hands through her hair and washed her face, then used J.P.'s toothbrush. She knew it was totally unhygienic, but morning breath would be so much grosser.

She exited J.P.'s bedroom suite and slowly navigated her way toward the downstairs study. There she found J.P. engrossed in a copy of *The Economist* and drinking his large mug of coffee. J.P. could be so *middle-aged* sometimes.

"Bo-ring," Jack announced, pulling away the magazine as she flopped onto the leather club chair next to him. Animal heads were mounted to the wall, in a lame attempt at British hunting lodge décor. Jack used to hate how everything in the Cashman Complexes was jumbled and over-the-top, with modern design sitting next to antiques next to whatever super expensive toy Dick Cashman had purchased. But by now, she was used to it, and the mishmash décor almost felt homey.

Roger, the Cashmans' British butler, glided into the room and offered her a glass of water, iced with lemon. Jack took it gratefully and sighed to herself. For all she knew, by next week she'd be living in some gross, water-stained apartment in Paris. It was too depressing to even think about.

"Looky what the cat dragged in!" Dick Cashman boomed as he entered the double doors on the other end of the room, trailed by two blond clipboard-holding women wearing matching Prada suits.

"Jeannette? Candice? This is my girl Jack," Dick said, thumping her on the back. Jack tried not to cough. "Jeannette and Candice are working with me to drum up some talk about our new outpost downtown." Dick winked. With his ruddy pink face, small cowboy hat, and tight pants, he looked like the jovial owner of some barbecue restaurant in Texas, not the wealthiest real estate mogul in New York. His latest property, the Cashman Lofts, was an eco-chic luxury building in Tribeca where everything was green.

"I didn't know you had a daughter," one of the women

murmured politely, extending an elegantly manicured hand in Jack's direction. Jack shook it weakly. She didn't want to entertain Dick's employees. All she wanted to do was crawl under J.P.'s Asprey blanket and go back to sleep.

"She's not my daughter—although she will be in a few years! She's my son's little lady," Dick explained. "Here, let's get some food in the breakfast nook!" Dick turned abruptly, leading them through the apartment and into an expansive Italian marble–floored kitchen. While the study looked like an English hunting lodge, the kitchen looked like it belonged in an airy Santa Monica bungalow. It was amazing that Dick was such a good real estate developer, since his personal taste was so off. "All right, let's sit!" he announced.

"Thanks so much for inviting me to breakfast, Dick." Jack smiled through her teeth. Even after all these years, it felt weird calling someone's dad Dick.

"Are they working you too hard in your tutu classes?" Dick asked in concern once everyone was seated around the rugged wood table. "Or is my son not taking care of your needs? You don't look so good!" He squinted his bulbous eyes at Jack, as if trying to get a better look.

"I'm fine," Jack mumbled. She wondered why she'd ever agreed to have breakfast with J.P.'s family.

"Jack's upset because she found out her mom's moving to Paris," J.P. piped up helpfully. Jack glared at him mutinously. She certainly didn't want to get into her family's fucked-up life in front of all these people. It was bad enough trying to deal with it on her own. Roger poured coffee and plunked baskets of scones in the center of the table. Jack wondered if there was some way she could excuse herself without seeming totally rude.

"Moving?" Dick Cashman bellowed as his wife, Tatyana, walked in, carrying two tiny puggles in her arms. Tatyana was a Russian ex-supermodel who'd gained fifty pounds since her prime and now had absurd cleavage. She was clad in a silk red kimono, but her hair was in an updo and she was wearing way too much red lipstick, as if she were about to present at an awards show, circa 1988.

"Who eez moving?" she asked in her heavy accent as she took a scone from the center of the table and stuffed it into her mouth. Crumbs stuck to her bright red lipstick and one of the dogs whined, clearly hoping to get a bite.

"My mother is moving to Paris for work and expects me to come with her," Jack explained, wanting to stab J.P. with a fork for bringing it up.

"Moving to Paris? Jackie, baby, you can't leave New York. You *are* New York." Dick winked for what felt like the twentieth time in ten minutes. Suddenly his face turned even pinker. He clapped his hands together. "You know, we're using the penthouse of the Cashman Lofts as a showroom, and what better way to add some glamour to the shack than with a pretty little lady?"

"She eez perfect." Tatyana appraised Jack as if she were a racehorse, leaning in to look at Jack's face. Jack tried not to cough from the cloyingly overbearing scent of her spicy perfume. "She could be the face of Cashman Lofts. Elegance and modernity. Zat is zee point? She is zee girl!"

Jack blinked. What were they talking about? Why would a building need a face?

"It could work." Candice nodded to Jeannette. Or Jeannette nodded to Candice. It was impossible to tell, since they both had shoulder-length, blown-dry hair, Botoxed foreheads, and super-bony collarbones. The two women pulled out their BlackBerrys and began typing frantically.

"Well, what do you think, Jackie baby? Want to move in? Be the face of the green movement?"

Jack looked at Dick in disbelief. He wanted her to live in the Cashman Lofts? She wouldn't have to move to Paris with her dramatic, crazy mother?

"I'd love to," Jack said smoothly. She resisted the urge to hug everyone, even J.P.'s fat, weird mom and Dick's robo-assistants.

"Great, great. It'll be great. We'll call Page Six, *New York*, *Harper's*, *Metropolitan* and get them over here. Show them the new face of green living in New York. It'll be *very* hot." Jeannette rubbed her hands together. Jack nodded giddily.

"Atta girl!" Dick clapped his hands in approval. "Now that that's settled, let's get some food on the table!" he commanded. Almost immediately, Roger and a bevy of other people came out of the kitchen carrying silver platters piled high with eggs, pancakes, and fresh fruit. Jack grinned. She could *definitely* get used to this.

"Guess what we're going to do when I move in," Jack whispered to J.P., once Tatyana and Dick were safely digging into their omelets and Candice and Jeannette were huddled over their BlackBerries. She was glad she'd gotten too drunk to do it last night. They'd do it once she moved into the lofts. It would be a perfect way to begin her perfect new life. And the best part about it was, it was all *free*.

You know what they say: Nothing comes without a price. . . .

r is for really pathetic

"Rhys, darling, are you okay?" Lady Sterling popped her head into Rhys's room on Saturday afternoon. With her ramrod-straight posture, elegantly white hair, and unlined face, she looked like a wig-wearing Nicole Kidman.

"Yep," Rhys murmured. In truth, he'd woken up an hour ago and wished more than anything he could fall back asleep. In times like this, most other kids would head straight to their parents' supply of Ambien. But most other kids didn't have a mom like Lady Sterling, the hyper-energetic hostess of the hit manners and culture show *Tea with Lady Sterling*. Cheerfulness and making the best of things were her personal religion.

"Are you sure?" Lady Sterling lifted her nose in the air like a German shepherd sniffing out trouble. Rhys glanced up unenthusiastically. Sitting up required way too much energy. His flat-screen TV in the corner was tuned to a baseball game, the Yankees versus the Red Sox. Not like Rhys gave a fuck who won.

Because on Channel Rhys, it's all Sterling versus Carlyle, all the time.

"Yeah, fine." Rhys pushed himself off his bed and brushed wordlessly past his mom. He sat down at his messy, book-strewn desk and turned on his Mac Air. Maybe his mom would think he was doing homework and leave him alone. "I might be getting a cold or something. I'm probably contagious," he lied.

"Rhys, darling, you're not fine. Anyone can see you're in crisis. You quit the swim team."

Rhys sighed and shook his head, wishing for the millionth time he could have parents like Hugh's, who spent most of their time at the opera or at their country house in Provence. Instead, his mom enjoyed prying into every single aspect of his life, eager to uncover some type of trend that she could break on her show, usually with him as a guest star. In the past, it had been tolerable because Kelsey would often join him in the segments. For one show they'd tried out trapeze lessons on the West Side, and in another, he'd demonstrated helpful lifesaving techniques in the Sterlings' basement pool. But now the only segments he could film were "How to Be a Loser" or "How to Not Notice When Your Best Friend Is Hooking Up with Your Girlfriend."

"Your father and I were talking," Lady Sterling continued, her eyebrows knitted together in concern. "You need something to revive you after the recent Kelsey upset. We're heading to London next weekend for Cousin Elfie's wedding, and maybe you should come. There will be some beautiful young ladies there." Lady Sterling nodded, no doubt thinking of the far-flung branches of their family tree.

Isn't that still, um, gross?

In fact, despite her accent, Lady Sterling was from Greenwich, Connecticut, and not Greenwich, UK, but everyone, including some of their more distant cousins, seemed to forget that. Most believed it was Lady Sterling herself—and not her husband, the thin, unassuming Algernon Sterling—who was directly descended from royalty. "I think your second cousin Jemimah is fifteen or sixteen. And I heard she just got her braces off, so I'm sure she looks lovely," Lady Sterling cooed.

"What?" Rhys glanced up sharply, the thought of dating one of his cousins finally tapping his brain awake. "And wait, how do you know about Kelsey?" He squinted at his mom. He hadn't said anything about it for precisely this reason.

"Kelsey called to tell me. But what would young love be without drama? Without intrigue, without the chase? Rhys, I can see that this is a formative moment for you." Lady Sterling beamed as she stalked across to the windows and flung open the drawn shades. "What we need to do, darling, is sit down and figure out how to win her back." Rhys cradled his head in his hands and sighed. So while Kelsey was sleeping with his ex–best friend, she was also buddy-buddy with his mom?

Lady Sterling perched on the edge of Rhys's bed, picking up his English notebook from a pile on the hardwood floor. "Shall we begin brainstorming?" she asked expectantly, flipping to a blank page.

Suddenly, Rhys's expansive bedroom felt tiny, and everything— from the framed photos on the wall of him and Kelsey kissing in Central Park to the pile of dusty swimming medals he had haphazardly strewn on his bookshelf—reminded him of who he used to be. Now he wasn't even sure who he was.

"I'm going for . . . a walk," he muttered, stuffing his black Lacroix wallet in his back pocket and grabbing his iPod. The last thing he needed was relationship advice from his mom.

"A brisk walk is good for circulation." Lady Sterling stood

up and crossed over to the door, nodding approvingly as if she'd come up with the idea herself. "Do you want me to come with you? This could be a great opener for the show. 'How to Break Up Without Breaking Down.' I can call David and see if the crew can get together."

"No thanks," Rhys said. His life was already pathetic. Seeing it play out on *Tea with Lady Sterling* would only make it worse.

Outside, Rhys finally felt like he could breathe. He turned and walked down Madison Avenue, not sure where he was even going. Normally he'd head down Fifth to be near the park, but he didn't want to take a chance at running into Kelsey, who lived at Seventy-seventh and Fifth.

He stuffed his hands into the pockets of his khakis. It was definitely fall. Last year, he and Kelsey used to spend hours wandering around the neighborhood, catching leaves as they fell from the trees that lined the sidewalks and stopping in the tiny cafés on Madison to share cappuccinos and napoleons. Kelsey was always impulsive and full of life. He tried to imagine his future without her. No swimming. No Kelsey. What would he do?

Please. This is Manhattan. There's always something—or someone—to do.

Once he safely passed Seventy-seventh Street he turned west and entered the park. He sat down on a bench near the East Lawn, where a group of guys were playing Hacky Sack in the center of the grass. That was where he and Kelsey used to go on picnics in the summer, where she would spend the afternoon lying on her stomach, reading Henry James novels and sketching. Even though he'd always lugged *Ulysses* or *Sons and Lovers* or another thick book to impress Kelsey, he'd spend most of the time watching her, sometimes running his hands through her silky strawberry blond hair.

Rhys watched the guys blissfully kick the Hacky Sack up and down in the afternoon sun. What was the point? There was no competition. Hacky Sack was so dumb. It wasn't a sport, it was a remedial activity for stoners who lacked the attention span and the muscles to play *real* sports. But they looked so . . . happy. Rhys knew he never looked happy when he swam. He looked stressed out and angry.

Suddenly, as if by silent agreement, the group wandered over to a large oak tree. Rhys saw one of the guys pull something from his pocket, light up, then pass it to the rest of the group. They were getting stoned. No one around seemed to mind, though. When they'd finished, they made their way back to their spot on the lawn. A few resumed the game, but two of them just lay down on their backs, looking up at the sky.

Rhys awkwardly plopped down from the bench onto the grass and lay back too. He knew it was sort of gay, but he wanted to see what the stoners *saw*. The sky was a beautiful, cerulean blue, but there was one large, gray-flecked cloud, right over him. Figured.

He stood up and brushed the grass off his Hugo Boss khakis. Just then, the Hacky Sack sailed through the air and thwacked him on the head.

"Ow!" Rhys rubbed his head. That *hurt*.

"Sorry, man!" one of the stoner guys yelled. "A little help?" He held up his hand, ready to accept the Hacky Sack. Rhys picked up the weird little ball of hemp. Whatever. He dropped it onto the arch of his limited edition John Varvatos Converse and kicked the ball toward the guys. As the ball sailed into the air, Rhys lost his balance and landed on his back. Hard.

He blinked his eyes. The same ominous cloud was above him, and his back fucking hurt. He cautiously pushed himself to a sitting position. At least he hadn't broken anything. Although it might have been better if he had. Then he could lie in a hospital bed and feel miserable without anyone judging him.

"Man, are you okay? That was the worst Hacky wipeout I've ever seen."

Rhys blinked. A Birkenstock-wearing guy was frowning down at him. He wore a tight yellow T-shirt with a picture of a smiling whale that read A WHALE OF A TIME IN WASHINGTON. His dirty brown hair was clumped into greasy-looking dreadlocks, and he had a silver nose ring that glinted in the sun.

"I'm fine," Rhys snapped harshly. He felt himself turning red. The Hacky Sack wipeout was further evidence he couldn't do *anything* right. He unsteadily stood up. "Bye," he added, giving the guy a weird half handshake, half fist bump. He felt like he had won the Dumb Asshole of the Year award.

"Relax, bro!" the guy yelled behind him.

"I'm fine," Rhys repeated as he shuffled toward the winding path out of the park. He awkwardly rubbed his head. Maybe he'd get as far as Seventy-seventh Street and collapse right under the green awning of Kelsey's building. She'd take him in and nurse him back to health and promptly forget about that fuckwad Owen Carlyle.

Or maybe he needs to get checked for a concussion.

o and *k* redefine intimate seating

One if by Land, Two if by Sea was a restaurant housed in what used to be the carriage house of Aaron Burr's seventeenth-century colonial home. It was on Barrow Street, a narrow, cobblestone street in the Village. It wasn't trendy, but it was definitely couple-friendly. And completely not his scene, Owen realized as he placed his hand on the small of Kelsey's back and escorted her from the cab into the narrow doorway. Owen preferred sticky-floored dive bars with beer specials and burgers for under five dollars. He'd never really understood why people were so averse to fast food chains. Hadn't anyone ever been to In-N-Out Burger in California? That shit was so good he'd marry it.

A french fry is forever?

"Aw, this is so sweet!" Kelsey exclaimed as they stood next to the narrow oak bar, adjusting the strap of her chocolate brown dress so it would stop falling down. She whirled around and gave Owen a kiss.

"Name?" an ancient, skinny guy at the reservation desk asked uncomfortably. Obviously, the restaurant wasn't used to having teenagers on a date. Neither was Owen. Somehow, it seemed more natural for the two of them to be naked, in his bed, than all dressed up at a fancy restaurant.

"Carlyle." Owen cleared his throat and loosened his blue Armani tie slightly. Avery had made him wear a jacket, and he felt *very* buttoned up. "Owen Carlyle."

"Right this way." The maître d' motioned for them to follow him up a rickety set of stairs and into a muted, dark-wood dining room, complete with faded Oriental rugs and exposed redbrick walls. Kelsey giggled, poking Owen and gesturing at a man who seemed half asleep over his chocolate soufflé. His oblivious, skinny wife continued to chat to the couple next to them.

Owen smiled and shook his head in disbelief. How typical of Avery to recommend a restaurant that was perfect for a seventy-fifth anniversary dinner. He just hoped they didn't have senior citizen–size portions. "Here you are." The host escorted them to a small, white linen–covered table in the corner. As he left, he snatched up the wine list, making a point that he knew exactly how young they were. A single rose and a dripping red candle adorned the table.

"Thanks again for planning this, Owen. This was a great idea." Kelsey smiled, displaying her adorably imperfect crooked left incisor. Owen instantly wanted to kiss her. Why couldn't they be on Kelsey's antique sleigh bed, or on his rooftop terrace, or in their special spot in Central Park . . . ?

"So, how's swimming?" Kelsey smiled sheepishly, as if she were trying to drag her mind away from the same dirty thoughts Owen was having.

"It's all right," Owen began. He focused on the slight hint of cleavage busting out of her dress. Her skin was sparkly. Owen always noticed that about girls. If he hadn't lived with Avery, he would have assumed it was totally natural, rather than courtesy of Benefit's Kitten Goes to Paris sparkling body powder.

"Tell me about it! I want to know *everything* about you." Kelsey raised her blondish eyebrow at him as a gray-haired waiter shuffled over to the table and delivered the menus.

"Good evening. Would you like to hear the specials?" the waiter asked in a bored voice. He looked like he was at least one hundred years old.

"Of course, we're always up for specials," Kelsey said teasingly, biting her adorable coral-colored lower lip. Owen felt her fingertips lightly dance over his leg.

Sea bass, char-grilled salmon . . . as the waiter rattled off the list, Owen tried to ignore Kelsey's fingertips drumming his knee. At this rate, he wasn't sure he could last the whole meal.

Down, boy! Patience is a virtue.

"I'll have the sea bass," Kelsey said agreeably. The waiter winked at her, showing more life than he had in the past five minutes.

"Me too," Owen agreed hurriedly, not even sure what they had ordered. Who *cared* about food?

"So, where were we?" Kelsey pulled her hand away and Owen felt a surge of disappointment. "Swimming . . ."

"Yeah." Owen nodded. He still wasn't sure if he wanted to tell Kelsey about making captain. It would just remind her of Rhys, and then they'd both feel shitty—again—for what had happened. But she was going to find out eventually. "I was actually made captain. Rhys quit." There.

"Rhys quit?" A frown crossed Kelsey's face, but was quickly replaced by a sunny smile. "Well, that's awesome for you! Congrats."

"Yeah," Owen agreed, unsure what else to say. There was so much he didn't know about her. He knew she went to Seaton Arms, that she was a fabulous kisser, that she had a gorgeous antique sleigh bed and a gorgeous body. . . and that was pretty much it. "So, do you do any sports? Or clubs?" he asked lamely.

"Tennis, remember?" Kelsey said teasingly.

"Of course!" Owen exclaimed like an idiot. *Right.* He'd stopped by her apartment a few days ago and she'd worn a flirty white skirt that hit mid-thigh, her strawberry blond bangs adorably pushed back by her visor.

"I mean, that was a dumb question. I guess, what I wanted to know was, what other stuff you like to do?" Owen stumbled.

"You first!" Kelsey exclaimed. "You're the one who wanted to have a sit-down dinner. Tell me something I don't know." She shrugged and smiled.

Thankfully, their salads arrived just then. Owen glanced down at the mix of greens on his plate. He racked his brain but couldn't come up with one interesting thing to say. He'd read an article in the paper the other day about how polar bear communities were shrinking, but that suddenly seemed extremely lame to bring up. He took a large bite of salad.

"I'm going to the ladies' room—maybe you could help me find it?" Kelsey's eyes danced mischievously as she scraped her wooden chair back.

"Of course." Was Kelsey suggesting what he *thought* she was suggesting? Owen stood up so fast the walnut chair practically clattered to the floor. Together, they wove their way through the maze of tables and down the stairs, ignoring the curious stares of other diners.

"I think it's this way," Kelsey said, taking Owen's hand and leading him toward a door near the bar. Owen squeezed her hand, his heart racing.

"Come in with me!" Kelsey said in a sexy whisper. Owen didn't hesitate. He followed her inside, quickly pulling the door closed. The bathroom was lit by several candles, making it seem almost romantic. He pushed her up against a wall and kissed her hard on the lips. It was exciting and explosive and romantic, like the first time they met. Kelsey kissed back hungrily, then bit into the shoulder of his white button-down shirt.

Suddenly, a knock on the door echoed through the bathroom. Kelsey and Owen froze, their eyes locked. And then they started kissing harder than ever.

"Get out immediately!" a stern female voice called as the doorknob rattled. Busted. But it only turned Owen on more. He pulled the strap of Kelsey's dress down her shoulders, exposing her creamy white skin.

"Yes!" she moaned eagerly.

"No! Get out now!" the voice yelled.

"We've got to go." Owen pulled away reluctantly, then opened the door.

"Uh, we were . . ." Owen stammered as he found himself face-to-face with a bevy of waitstaff who'd all formed a huddle around the bathroom door.

Probably to protect the eyes of the senior citizen patrons.

"I was feeling sick," Kelsey explained as she brushed past a skinny, fifty-something waitress.

"You *are* sick," the waitress said, rolling her eyes.

"Please leave the premises immediately," the maître d' said as he weaved his way toward Owen and Kelsey. Owen nodded. He couldn't look at Kelsey because he knew if he did, they'd just start laughing.

And making out again?

"Follow me down the back stairs," the maître d' barked, thrusting Kelsey's large blue Marc Jacobs satchel toward her as if it were contaminated. "Now," he added, clapping his hand against Owen's shoulder.

"Sorry," Kelsey and Owen mumbled at the same time. The maître d' led them down a rickety staircase and to a nondescript door, holding it open.

"Out!" he growled.

"Of course, sir!" Owen said. He couldn't resist grabbing one of the roses from one of the unoccupied tables as he ushered Kelsey out onto the cobblestone side street.

Finally, they both burst out in laughter as the door closed with a thud.

"My lady?" Owen teased, holding out the slightly wilted rose toward Kelsey.

"My hero!" Kelsey said goofily as she accepted the flower. She stood on tiptoe to kiss him gently. Owen sighed in happiness. Maybe getting kicked out of a restaurant wasn't all that classy, but it was definitely fun. "Let's go somewhere more comfortable?" she asked hopefully.

Owen nodded giddily as he put his hand up to hail a cab. Avery was right. A date was a *great* idea. A taxi screeched to the curb, and, giggling, Kelsey scooted inside. Owen followed, squishing in next to her, their thighs touching.

"Seventy-second and Fifth." Owen gave his address, slipping his hand inside Kelsey's as she accidentally-on-purpose let the strap of her dress slide off her glittery shoulder.

That cabdriver is going to be in for a surprise.

gossipgirl.net

Disclaimer: All the real names of places, people, and events have been altered or abbreviated to protect the innocent. Namely, me.

hey people!

news flash

Unmentionables on the side of a bus? Old news. The *new* news is a larger-than-life billboard campaign, announcing the fabulous downtown Cashman Lofts. And the flawless face of those lofts is none other than our **J.** Surprised? I'm not. She's the crème de la crème, and she *always* rises to the top. Which brings us to . . .

climbing the ladder

For a city designed on a grid system and dotted with skyscrapers, is it any wonder New Yorkers are obsessed with knowing *exactly* where they are at all times? I'm not talking about the girls who BlackBerry message all of their acquaintances to let them know they're ordering coffee at EAT on Madison or trying on a Thakoon dress in Bergdorf's. I'm talking about knowing where we stand with our friends, our enemies, and everyone else who matters. It's human nature to want to know where you fit in. After all, how else would you know how much further you have to reach? But when you feel yourself shaking in your Sigerson Morrisons as you lift your foot onto the next rung, remember: It's better to be halfway up a desirable ladder than at the top of one you never wanted to climb in the first place.

sightings

O, standing alone and looking sad outside **Paragon Sports** . . . Somebody get stood up? At least until **K** showed up and proceeded to make out with him inside the store. What an, ahem, athletic couple! **A**, sneaking around the **Bliss** spa locker room after a Blissage 75 massage. Who's she avoiding this time? **B,** reading *I'm Okay, You're Okay* near those gross dollar bookshelves in front of the **Strand**. My verdict: *not okay*. **R** in a random touristy shop on St. Marks, looking at Hacky Sacks. New hobby? **J** seeing her mom off at JFK, then stepping into a Lincoln Town Car and being whisked down to **Industria** studios on Jane Street for a Cashman Lofts photo shoot. Smile for the camera!

your e-mail

 Dear Gossip Girl,
I'm a therapist and I'm worried that I am losing touch with my younger clients. Since you seem to be a bit of an expert in today's youth, please tell me what you think the dreams, desires, and goals are of your generation. Your answer may help millions of young and confused individuals!
—ListeningtoelephantsPhD

 Dear LE,
While I'm flattered to be considered an expert, I think you'd be better off going directly to the source—try reading your clients' blogs. Or just listening to them. Instead of, um, elephants.
—GG

One final word about climbing: The higher you go, the farther there is to fall. And sometimes, there's no net to catch you.

You know you love me.

gossip girl

j's lofty ambitions

"There." Jack adjusted an oversize framed photo of a pointe shoe on the wall near her new California king-size bed. In the artsy photograph the pink satin of the shoe looked almost sweet, while the scuffs on the toe proved how hard it had been pounded against the stage. It expressed everything she loved about ballet: how it was exactly the right balance of beauty and grit.

Sound familiar?

The intercom buzzed in a gentle, three-toned chime and the face of the Cashman Lofts doorman appeared on the grainy video feed.

"Hello?" Jack cradled the receiver against her shoulder, gazing at her surroundings. It was a world apart from the garret. The apartment was intended to be used as a showroom only, so it had already been decorated to hype up the aesthetic of the building: The loftlike space was painted muted grays, and was decorated by Gavin Palmer, an interior designer famous for making the green movement actually cool and livable. A chandelier made from recycled airplane parts hung over a long bamboo table, a multicolored silk and wool rug covered the polished free trade–

cork floor, and light streamed through a skylight and onto her organic cotton–sheeted bed at the opposite end of the room.

"Miss Jack, your guests are here," the doorman said.

"Send them up!" Jack announced regally, pulling her auburn hair back into a messy ponytail and rolling down the waistband of her black Stella McCartney for Adidas yoga pants. Finally, her life seemed to be falling into place. She'd dropped her mom off at the airport this morning, where Vivienne had acted ridiculous and dramatic as usual. But an embarrassing airport au revoir was a small price to pay for absolute freedom. Whenever Jack looked around the loft and realized it was *hers*, she just wanted to jump up and down on the bed in glee. She actually had, briefly, until she realized the sustainable bamboo might not be all that sturdy.

Besides, isn't there something *else* she should be doing on the bed?

After a brief photo shoot downtown for the lofts' new ad campaign, Jack had arrived at the building to find the penthouse apartment completely furnished. Of course, the first thing she did was invite Sarah Jane, Genevieve, and Jiffy over to see her new apartment. After all, they'd stuck by her when she'd been poor. She wanted them to see that she was back on top. She flung open the door in anticipation of their arrival, hurriedly pushing her Louis Vuitton suitcase under the bed. She hadn't even begun to unpack yet, but wasn't that what maids were for?

"Ohmigod!" Jiffy squealed, barreling into the apartment. She was trailed by Genevieve and Sarah Jane, each carrying an armful of packages and bags. "This is so cool! It's like you're all grown up! It's even better than Beatrice's place," she added as she walked toward the enormous picture windows in awe.

"Thanks," Jack said demurely, glancing around the loft like it was nothing special. But it really *was* sensational. "What's all that?" Jack frowned at the bags Sarah Jane and Genevieve piled onto the teak dining room table.

"I don't know." Genevieve shrugged and flipped her wavy blondish hair over her shoulder. "Your doorman told us to bring them up."

Jack greedily snatched a large red and yellow package and tore it open. A brand-new black Marc Jacobs purse was inside, along with a cream-colored envelope. She slid her finger under the flap.

Dear Jack,
    Just a little housewarming present. Think of us if you're in the area—would be happy to help you in any way possible.
    Love,
    Jane and the rest of the girls at Tender Heart

Jack smiled. Tender Heart was a cool boutique in Nolita where she'd loved to shop before she got cut off. They'd obviously heard about her new move. Her eyes flicked over to the pile of boxes. Were *all* of these presents?

And it's not even her birthday!

"Oh my God." Genevieve yanked the thick cardstock from Jack's hand. "I can't believe J.P. did this for you. When I was dating Breckin, he couldn't even get us into Area. On a *Tuesday*." She sighed, still not over the less-then-five-minute fling she'd had in L.A. over the summer with an actor in one of her dad's films.

"J.P. didn't do this for me. His *dad* did," Jack corrected, yanking the card out of Genevieve's hands and throwing it on the granite counter. Oops. That didn't sound quite right. "I mean, I met his dad's PR team and they decided that they wanted me to be the face of the lofts," Jack clarified.

"Still, they wouldn't have chosen you if you weren't J.P.'s girl-friend, right?" Jiffy asked, poking her head into the Sub-Zero refrigerator, thoughtfully stocked with Whole Foods groceries by one of the Cashman employees.

"Can you make me a cranberry vodka, Jif?" Jack asked, ignor-ing Jiffy's asinine question. Obviously it had *helped* that J.P.'s mom had suggested the idea, but it wasn't as if that was the only reason she'd become the face of the lofts.

Jiffy nodded absently, pulling out a handle of vodka from the freezer and a few of the brand-new Riedel glasses from one of the cupboards. She busily got to work on one of the slate countertops.

"You can open some of the mail and stuff if you want," Jack offered generously to Sarah Jane and Genevieve, who were both examining every corner of the apartment as if it were an estate sale. Sarah Jane picked up a soy candle and sniffed it, wrinkling her nose.

"Thanks." Genevieve's voice dripped sarcasm. Whatever.

Jack pretended not to notice and walked over to the sweep-ing windows, looking for the millionth time at the just-unveiled billboard. It was of her, wearing a flowy green Oscar de la Renta dress and admiring a daisy, as if she was just about to do that dumb *he loves me, he loves me not* thing with the petals. She looked dreamy and happy and in love. The caption on the bottom of the ad said, LIVE AND LOVE IN GREEN. It didn't totally make sense, but she didn't care. With the billboard flat against the lower Manhat-tan skyline, Jack peered down onto the city, its larger-than-life queen, benevolently watching the people below her.

She was *back*.

Sarah Jane sidled up next to her. "This really is awesome," she offered, still holding one of the dumb candles she'd picked up from a side table. "And it's all organic?" She glanced skeptically at a leather club chair nestled below a dormer window. Sarah Jane's mom was the editor in chief of *Bella*, a fashion and décor magazine, so she always pretended to know about all the latest design trends.

"I guess." Jack shrugged. Who the fuck cared? "What else did I get?" She plopped down on a stool next to Genevieve and eagerly thumbed through the pile of brightly colored invites scattered against the black counter.

We are pleased to invite you and your guest to the premiere of . . .

Please come to drinks and dinner at Daniel in honor of . . .

The Whitney Museum and Vogue *magazine hope you will attend . . .*

"Get out your calendars, ladies!" Jack grinned, grabbing one of the vodka crans Jiffy had prepared and taking a long swig. She deserved it. "We have some parties to attend."

Glad to see the queen treating her subjects so nicely!

Just then, Jack heard footsteps outside the door. She narrowed her eyes at Jiffy, sure that she'd invited one of her lame sophomore friends over. Then a key scraped in the lock. *What the fuck?*

The door swung open, framing J.P. He was wearing neatly pressed khakis, a blue Thomas Pink button-down shirt, and a grin.

"What are you doing here?" Jack demanded. She cringed. She hadn't meant to sound that bitchy and accusatory, it was just that she had planned to spend the afternoon showing off a little bit in front of her friends, and she couldn't really do that with J.P. here.

"This looks great. My dad was telling me how excited everyone is about the campaign." J.P. gave her a kiss.

"Your dad gave you a key?" she asked, surprised.

Before J.P. could answer, Henry, the doorman, appeared with two Tumi duffel bags slung over each shoulder.

"Here you go, sir," he announced grandly to J.P., depositing them at his feet.

"Are you moving in?" Jack asked sharply.

Jiffy pushed her long brown bangs out of her eyes and stared at him curiously.

"What, you don't want me?" J.P. teased, hauling the bags over toward the bed. "I just thought I'd leave some stuff here. Better than taking cabs all the time. Bad for the environment." J.P. winked.

Jack nodded, unsure of what to think. Living by herself in a cool, unsupervised, furnished apartment was one thing, but living with her boyfriend whom she just got back together with was something totally different. She wasn't sure if she was ready for J.P. to see her eating cookie dough straight out of the tube and watching crappy television. Plus, they'd have to share a bathroom. That didn't seem very romantic at all.

"What are you girls doing?" J.P. eased onto one of the stainless steel bar stools lined up against the slate counter.

"Toasting the new apartment," Genevieve explained, taking a liberal swig of her cranberry vodka. "It's all thanks to you!" Genevieve cocked her glass at J.P., but smiled at Jack, her lips already stained by her drink.

Jack shot her a death stare back. Hadn't she *just* told Genevieve that J.P. was *not* the reason she had the lofts campaign? Had Genevieve developed vodka-induced amnesia?

"Thanks!" J.P. said companionably, grabbing the glass proffered by Jiffy. Jack sulkily grabbed it out of J.P.'s hand and downed it. At least when she was drinking, she didn't have to talk. Because she had quite a few things to say to J.P. Wasn't he supposed to say how gorgeous and talented she was, and point out that *that* was the reason his dad's PR people wanted her to do the campaign?

"You okay, Jack?" J.P. asked, opening the freezer to get some fresh ice. He seemed totally fucking at home in the apartment, hanging out with all her friends.

"Perfect," Jack said crisply. Right now, all she wanted was for everyone to go home so she could just stand at the picture window and gaze at her billboard.

We all have our hobbies.

There was another knock at the door. Jack sighed loudly as she skulked over to open it. It was probably J.P.'s parents, ready to move in too.

Instead, it was Henry. He was holding a tiny, dingy white dog. It was desperately wiggling out of Henry's arms, obviously terrified to have its four legs so far off the ground.

"Here you go," Henry announced, setting the dog on the floor. He hastily retreated as the dog ran over to Jack, its toenails clicking against the floor. Immediately, it began humping her leg.

"Cuuuuute!" Jiffy and Sarah Jane exclaimed at the same time. Jack not-so-subtly kicked the tiny animal away from her leg.

"Oooh, look!" Jiffy exclaimed, untying a pink ribbon from the dog's collar.

"It's from my mom," J.P. explained, taking the note from Jiffy and holding it out toward Jack.

Jack smiled tightly as she grabbed the note. Tatyana had actually placed a maroon-lipsticked kiss on the front. Jack gingerly opened the envelope without touching the kiss mark, as if Tatyana's tackiness could be transferred through her '80s matte lipstick.

A dog as beautiful as my son's woman! A million kisses in your new home, read the note. English was Tatyana's second language, but it sort of sounded like she was likening Jack to the gross, obviously oversexed little monster.

"It's a maltipoo," J.P. explained helpfully.

Jiffy cooed idiotically, sliding down on the floor to pet the dog. Maybe Jiffy could just take it once J.P. left.

"Let's think of a name," J.P. said, grabbing Jack's hand. Jack softened slightly. Yes, everything was supremely fucking weird right now, but the main thing was that J.P. loved her. Maybe living together wouldn't be so bad. It'd just make it that much easier to have s-e-x whenever they wanted. It might be fun, actually. It could be perfect.

"We can do that later." Jack smiled, trying to ignore her feeling of restlessness. After all, it had been a long day.

"Right, I guess we should probably take her outside. Let her get to know the neighborhood. I'd like to look around too," J.P. said eagerly.

Jack nodded, her good mood flicking off like a light switch. Maybe he could take Genevieve, Sarah Jane, and Jiffy with him.

And the little dog, too.

street of dreams

"There she is!" A giggly sophomore's voice wafted through the door and into Mr. Beckham's darkened classroom on Monday at noon. Avery glared over at the tiny window in the wooden doorway. This was the fourth time class had been interrupted by a gaggle of ridiculous underclassmen desperately trying to catch a glimpse of Jack Laurent, as if she were a *real* celebrity rather than a classmate who just so happened to have her photo in a dumb real estate advertising campaign.

Avery glanced over at Mr. Beckham, hoping he'd chase them away, but his eyes were affixed to the screen. They were all *supposed to* be watching *The Dreamers*, a totally dirty Bertolucci film about a brother, sister, and best friend doing it everywhere in 1960s Paris. Of course, Jack and her bitchtastic friends weren't even *pretending* to watch the movie, instead giggling over Jack's picture in the *New York Post*. It was totally unfair.

This morning, Jack's freckled face had been on all the gossip blogs and all the newspapers, and all anyone wanted to do was talk to her about her stupid billboard—which, thank *God*, was only downtown. Still, even the tiny postage stamp–size black and white picture of the billboard that was inset on Page Six was too much. Jack looked like a fucking *supermodel*. And she knew it.

Finally, the bell rang. Jack swished past Avery's desk, accidentally-on-purpose bumping into it so that Avery's empty Evian water bottle fell on the floor.

"Sorry," Jack murmured, not sounding sorry at all. "See you at lunch," she added, making the statement sound like a threat. Avery stared miserably at the empty water bottle on the floor. Even though all the Constance students were treating Jack like she could do no wrong, it was clear she hadn't forgotten her mission to make Avery's life hell in any and every way possible. The rest of the class filed out, hustling in Jack's wake.

Avery gathered her things and glanced around the empty classroom. The last thing she felt like doing was heading to the cafeteria and facing Jack and her entourage. "Can I help you with anything, sir?" Avery asked Mr. Beckham.

"Umph," he grunted. He was futilely trying to wrestle the disc from the DVD player, and, like any teacher over thirty-five, had no idea what he was doing.

"Sir?' Avery pressed, her frustration growing. She couldn't believe Mr. Beckham was ignoring her. It wasn't like she really wanted to hang out with her gross film teacher during lunch.

"No, that's okay, Ms. Carlyle," Mr. Beckham said, not bothering to look up.

"*Please?*" Avery pleaded. "I mean, I'd love to help you in any way possible," she amended, not wanting to sound too desperate. Jack always made a point of publicly accosting her in the cafeteria, and she didn't even want to know what she'd do now that everyone was treating her like a fucking rock star. Avery had spent all *last* week discussing books with Mrs. McLean and some of the Constance overseer ladies during lunch. This week they were supposed to start *Anna Karenina*, but she'd begged off. Although maybe she'd made the wrong choice. Reading Russian novels with the headmistress sounded like a vacation compared to facing Jack and her minions in all their bitchy, cafeteria-dominating glory.

"Well . . ." Mr. Beckham turned around and appraised Avery, his mouth cracking into a creepy grin. He winked lecherously at her, as if the film had given him ideas. "Maybe you could help me in the darkroom? I have some developing to do for my afternoon photography class."

"Actually, I'm not really good at photography," Avery lied, quickly exiting the classroom and hustling through the hall. She glanced thoughtfully out one of the second-floor windows onto the tree-lined street below. It wasn't too cold today. Maybe she could grab a yogurt and just sit outside somewhere.

Steeling her courage, Avery marched into the blond wood–beamed cafeteria. She subtly glanced around, looking for a friendly face. Everyone seemed to have their heads down, engaged in conversation with their friends. At this point, she'd kill to have lunch with Baby, even though sitting together made it obvious they didn't have any other friends. But she didn't spot her sister's tangled hair anywhere.

"I heard she was trying to pay Mr. Beckham to date her. Of course he said no," Sarah Jane Jenson whispered lazily to Jiffy as she daintily swirled a spoon through her cup of zero percent–fat Greek yogurt.

"I know. She's already called all these male-escort services, but they turned her down because she's underage. Maybe she should just become a lesbian," Jiffy replied as she pushed her shaggy brown bangs out of her eyes.

"Unless she *is* a total lesbo with that weirdo, Sydney," Sarah Jane remarked loudly enough so Avery could hear. Avery stood there stupidly, feeling like she'd been knifed in the heart. These girls used to be her friends, and on the surface, they still looked so sweet. Something about Jiffy's freckly, heart-shaped face had always seemed so friendly.

Looks can be deceiving.

"Hi Avery," Genevieve yelled from farther down the table, glancing up from her Treo. Sarah Jane and Jiffy giggled as if the greeting were the most amusing thing they'd ever heard. Avery willed herself not to look over at them as she made her way to the cafeteria line.

"Blackmail anyone lately?"

Avery turned to find Jack Laurent towering above her. Even though she was wearing her Constance seersucker skirt and a boatneck Loro Piana black sweater, Jack looked even more flawless than on her stupid billboard. Avery felt hives begin to form on her chest. It always happened when she was upset.

"Hi Jack," Avery mumbled, trying to sidestep her, but Jack effortlessly stepped in the same direction. Avery narrowed her blue eyes. What did Jack want?

A rumble?

"Ignore the Billboard Bitch."

Avery felt an arm clasp her elbow from behind. She whirled around to see Sydney Miller, Baby's all black–wearing, pierced-nipple friend. Today she wore a super-faded Third Rail T-shirt under her wrinkly Constance blazer and high-top Converse that looked like they'd belonged to some really unhygienic guy in the 1980s.

"Hi." Avery wasn't sure if she should be happy about being

rescued from a Jack showdown, or feel bad about being rescued by *Sydney*.

"Avery and I have somewhere to go. You know, some advertisements to deface?" Sydney grinned wickedly at Jack. "Corporate slut," she hissed, tugging on Avery's elbow.

Avery allowed Sydney to steer her firmly out of the cafeteria, through the royal blue doors of Constance, and onto the street.

"Thanks," Avery mumbled once they were safely outside.

"No problem," Sydney shrugged. "God, what a bitch. Want to grab some food? I'm sort of in the mood for falafel."

Not bothering to wait for a reply, Sydney made her way toward the shiny street vendor cart on the corner. Street food? Avery wrinkled her nose. But she didn't really have a choice. It wasn't like she could go back in the cafeteria, and her stomach was growling. The last thing she needed was to faint during AP English and have everyone assume she was anorexic.

Sydney triumphantly returned, holding up two foil-wrapped pouches.

"Think fast!" She threw the package in Avery's general direction. Avery automatically held her hands up to catch it.

"Thanks." She unwrapped the steaming foil package. Two falafel balls were nestled into a piece of pita surrounded by gooey strings of iceberg lettuce. They looked like clumps of fried dirt. Gross.

"Look, Sydney," she began awkwardly. She might as well let Sydney know she appreciated her gesture.

"Is this one of those speeches where now that you realize you have no friends, you want to let me know you're a better person?" Sydney grinned and Avery could see her tongue piercing flash in the midday sun. "I don't need to hear that shit. I like your sister, and I think you have some potential underneath that two hundred–dollar headband." Sydney shrugged, biting into her falafel.

"Thanks," Avery said in confusion. Sydney made her feel like she was just as shallow and bitchy as Jack.

"Hey, no problem." Sydney paused, mid-bite, and squinted at the royal blue doors. "Isn't that your sister? Hey bitch!" She yelled cheerily.

"Oh my God, I haven't seen you in forever!" Baby squealed, warmly hugging Sydney. "You totally saved my ass with the *Rancor* project. I owe you. I'll get you *anything*. Another piercing? A tattoo?" Baby offered. Suddenly, her eyes flicked over to Avery's untouched lunch. "Yum!" Baby pulled the pita out of Avery's hand and bit into it hungrily.

"Another tattoo might be nice." Sydney seemed to seriously consider Baby's offer. "Want to go now?"

"I have to go to therapy." Baby shrugged. "I'm trying a new lady. But maybe after, I'll call you?" she asked. "I've always wanted a fish on my foot."

"What are you doing here?" Avery interrupted, glaring at her sister. And since when did Baby want a tattoo?

Maybe since she'd embarked on her journey of the mind?

"Brilliant!" Sydney nodded to Baby. "It works on so many levels. And good for you for going to therapy. My mom's a therapist, and she's always after Mrs. McLean to sponsor these lame team-building workshops in the woods."

"I should probably leave soon. I don't want to be late, you know?" She scanned the street for any empty cabs, taking another bite of Avery's sandwich.

"Maybe you do." Sydney shrugged, her mouth full of falafel.

"My mom always said our subconscious is a manipulative little fucker," Sydney observed, turning to Avery. "That's why, even though you hate it, you're so going to be best friends with Jack Laurent. You'll probably be the maid of honor at her wedding, maybe have a completely tortured affair of the mind with her fiancé. But you wouldn't go through with it." Sydney smiled, obviously pleased with Avery's falling expression.

"I'm going to go." Avery stalked back inside the doors of Constance.

"Oh hey, don't be mad! I'm sorry!" Sydney called after her, clearly not sorry. She turned to Baby. "I love fucking with your sister. It's so easy!" she marveled.

Baby grinned, nodding. Sydney was such a straight-shooting, *what you see is what you get* girl that spending time with her made Baby remember a time in her own life when things weren't so complicated. When she wasn't hauled into the headmistress's office every week, when no one made fun of her outfits, when being adventurous wasn't seen as being psychologically damaged. Baby sighed, her mood suddenly darkening.

"You need to go," Sydney said, as if noticing Baby's sudden shift in attitude. A lone cab that had been idling on the corner immediately pulled up to the curb. "Call me when you're done. I can't wait to get inked!"

Baby smiled and got into the cab. It wasn't a bad idea. Maybe getting a tattoo could be a cathartic experience.

You are what you ink?

b one with nature

Baby slid into the cracked black vinyl seat of the yellow cab, realizing as soon as it squealed away from the curb that she still held Avery's sandwich in one hand.

"Where to?" The greasy-haired cabbie craned his neck through the Plexiglas partition as if he were going to yell at Baby for eating in the cab, then decided against it when he saw her Constance uniform. His face cracked into a grin. "You skipping school?"

Baby pulled the wrinkled ad from her lime green Brooklyn Industries bag and smoothed it against her thighs. "Number eight Jane Street." She ignored the cabbie as he winked into the rearview, and slumped into the seat, watching the dorky broadcast about the wonders of New York on the cab's tiny screen. In this segment, a white-haired lady with a British accent was going on and on about the joys of rooftop gardens. Baby clicked the volume to mute and looked down again at the advertisement. *Ophelia Ravenfeather, Life Healer*, the ad read in loopy purple script. It didn't have a photograph, featuring instead an abstract illustration of a calm pond filled with smiling goldfish.

Baby gazed out the window. The stately buildings on Fifth turned into the overwhelming skyscrapers of Midtown, then finally the cute brownstones in the West Village. The sidewalks were surprisingly busy for early afternoon, filled with people enjoying the sunny fall day.

Her heart thumped against her chest as the cabbie turned onto Jane Street, a winding, cobblestone street in the Village that looked more like a street in Barcelona than Manhattan. She felt a pang of nostalgia for Spain. Maybe she should have just stayed. People were friendly there. She could set up shop in a café and teach English to people in exchange for food. She'd spend her nights sleeping on the beach. It'd be perfect.

Until she got bored two weeks later and hopped a flight to Morocco, of course.

"Here we go," the cabbie announced, squealing to a stop in front of a nondescript four-story brownstone.

"Thanks!" Baby squeaked. She pulled out a twenty from her wallet, which was made of duct tape; a gift her stoner ex-boyfriend in Nantucket made for her. Unlike the relationship, it was indestructible. "Keep the change," she added.

Crossing her fingers for luck, she hurried up the uneven stairs of the building and rang buzzer number twenty-two. No answer. She rang again.

"I'm coming down," a frantic voice called loudly into the speaker. On the sidewalk, two well-groomed guys and their tiny poodles looked over in curiosity. "Don't go anywhere!" the voice commanded.

"Okay!" Baby yelled uncertainly back into the speaker. She shifted from one foot to the other. The town house was only a block away from Hudson River Park, and she could just make out the grayish blue water of the Hudson. She breathed deeply. Ever since she was little, the sight of water relaxed her.

Suddenly, two hands grabbed Baby's shoulder.

"Ah!" she yelled involuntarily. She whirled around, expecting to be eye to eye with a knife, or a gun barrel, or . . . a gray-haired lady wearing yoga pants and a North Face red fleece jacket who came up to her chin?

Fleece *can* be terrifying.

"I apologize," the woman said, placing her hands on Baby's shoulders again as if nothing had happened. "I'm your healer." She appraised Baby with her muddy brown eyes. She didn't *look* like a healer. With her chapped lips, flyaway gray hair, and red hands, she reminded Baby of one of her mom's friends who worked on an organic communal farm in Vermont. The triplets used to go every year and help her during apple-picking season.

"My name is Ophelia Ravenfeather, but since we'll be working together, I think it's important for my clients to come up with their own name for me," she said expectantly, taking a step closer to Baby so that they were both balanced on the same narrow step.

Baby smiled uncertainly. This was actually weirder than she'd anticipated, but who was she to judge? At least it was better than being in a clinical, all-white office.

"I'm supposed to pick a name for you?" Baby repeated. Near them, a couple walked by with their golden retriever. Maybe it was a weird psychological thing, but she'd been noticing *a lot* of dogs lately. They always brought back memories of how much fun it had been at the very beginning of the year to walk J.P. Cashman's puggles. That was before they'd hooked up. She sighed in frustration. Maybe she should just forget about boys and adopt a dog.

There's one high-maintenance maltipoo who might need a new home. . . .

"Yes. What would you like to call me? One of my clients calls me Friend, one calls me The Big H, one calls me Grandma—it just depends." Ophelia smiled encouragingly.

"Um, I don't know." Baby considered, racking her brain for something that wouldn't sound totally weird. Was this some sort of psychological test?

And what are this woman's credentials?

"I guess just Ophelia for now?" Baby asked haltingly.

"Okay, for now. But once we get more comfortable with each other, I expect a name," Ophelia said in a warning tone. "And I see your aura. It's . . ." A dark cloud seemed to cross over her wrinkled, weather-beaten face. She shook her head. "Never mind. At least your chakras are working. Mostly." She added cryptically.

"Um, thanks." Baby smiled hesitantly. She pulled out the wrinkled form Mrs. McLean had given her to get signed for each hour of therapy. "So, as I mentioned, I've been recommended to do twenty hours of therapy. I really liked your ad and I think I'm on the same page as you, but I'd love if you could tell me a little bit about what we'll be doing in the sessions?"

Ophelia took the form, frowned at it, then shoved it back at Baby. "We'll deal with that later. For now, we need to get to the park. I have *a lot* of work to do with you," she said ominously. With that, Ophelia ran down the steps, showing a surprising amount of energy for a senior citizen. Baby trailed behind. So, did that mean Ophelia *would* sign the form? And why were they going to the park?

Ophelia hurried her down the street and across the paved bike path, finally reaching the narrow grassy strip that was the Hudson River Park. It was filled with picnickers, bikers, and joggers enjoying the afternoon sunshine. On the river, boats were bobbing in the water as if expressly for the viewing pleasure of the nearby picnickers. Baby smiled. This wouldn't be so bad.

"Okay." Ophelia clapped her hands as she reached a spot of grass. They stood dangerously close to a young couple enjoying a Dean & Deluca picnic. "This has good energy. Now, to begin with, let's do some downward dog." Instantly, she placed her gnarled hands on the ground and stuck her butt in the air.

"Um, I thought we were going to talk?" Baby asked. Starting off in a yoga pose was strange, even for her. What *was* this? Hippie healing 101?

"You don't need to talk to heal," Ophelia said mysteriously, standing up from her yoga pose, her face flushed. "Your turn," she said to Baby, motioning with her eyes for her to follow her lead. Baby cautiously pulled her Constance skirt down so she wouldn't flash everyone and set her hands on the ground.

"Hmm." Ophelia appraised her. "I think we need to go someplace else. Your energy isn't meshing well here. It's fighting me." She placed her thumb on her angular chin and stroked it gently. Baby could make out little coarse hairs sticking out of a mole on her face.

"I'll tell you what, Baby." Ophelia drew closer to her and placed her bony hand on Baby's shoulder. "You're going to close your eyes and walk until you find a place that feels right."

Baby closed her eyes, feeling like she was trapped in some sort of bizarre kindergarten class gone wrong, and began to walk. She paused and took a breath. She could feel the sun through her thin white Hanes tank top, and she could smell the faint scent of leaves burning somewhere in the far distance. Maybe she *did* just need to tune in. She took a few tentative steps.

"Yo, watch it, bitch!!"

Suddenly, Baby's shin made contact with something metallic and hard. Her eyes flew open in surprise. A man wearing neon-yellow bike shorts and a skintight black shirt lay sprawled on the bike path, a bright red bike on top of him. "I almost fucking hit you! What the hell are you doing?" he yelled as he stood up.

Well, she can cross that spot off the positive energy location list.

"I'm so sorry!" Baby picked up the guy's Ray-Ban sunglasses from the pavement. "Let me help you."

"Heal yourself first!" Ophelia barked, pulling Baby away from the bike.

"Sorry!" Baby called again to the biker in desperation.

"Well, I think we learned a lesson. You obviously were drawn to him, and see what happened?"

"I was walking around with my eyes closed!" Baby briefly lost patience.

"No. You were following your heart. And your heart led you into an entanglement with a man." Ophelia nodded sagely. "You need to tune in to yourself and stop getting tangled up with members of the opposite sex."

Baby stiffened, a chill running up her spine despite the sunny weather. Despite the hippietastic rhetoric, it was pretty much the same conclusion Dr. Janus had made: that Baby was overly dependent on guys.

"What can I do about it?" Baby asked, searching Ophelia's muddy brown eyes.

"First, we need to establish some rituals for you. Chanting, essential oils, a juice cleanse, things like that. We need you to learn that you can depend on yourself. So, let's begin!" Ophelia rubbed her hands together in glee. "I'll find a safe healing spot," she offered gallantly.

She led them over to an area of the park that jutted out into the water, out of the way of any bikers. Toddlers were playing on the lush lawn, watched over by nannies gossiping on wooden benches flanking the grass.

"Okay, close your eyes and imagine a word," Ophelia said. Suddenly, her mouth contorted into a grimace, as if she'd sucked on a lemon. "Actually, I don't think you're ready for eyes-closed work yet. Keep them open, but look down at the ground, concentrate on one blade of grass, and imagine a word."

Baby dutifully bowed her head, but the only words she could think of were weird, SAT-style words, like *perspicacious* and *fungible*. Those words didn't describe her at all, but no matter what, she couldn't think of any that *did*.

"Can you share your word?"

Baby's eyes flicked to the slow moving water. "Ocean?" She suggested lamely. She hoped that'd be okay. After all, wasn't this lady's whole deal all about finding your inner ocean?

"Wrong answer!" Ophelia barked, suddenly morphing from kindly grandmother to sadistic game show host. The nannies looked up and frowned at the noise. Baby smiled at them apologetically. "Try again. I can see the word *pulsating* from your aura," Ophelia urged.

Baby closed her eyes. The word *pulsate* made her think of *pulse*, which made her think of *heart*, which made her think of . . .

"Love?" Baby asked. "Love," she repeated firmly.

Ophelia shook her head sadly. "No, that's not it either. I can tell that with you, we need to get beyond words. I'm going to give you a chant. Are you ready?"

Baby nodded, even though it was clear that it didn't matter if she was ready or not. Ophelia stood up, closed her eyes and drew her hands together, as if she were praying, then balanced, flamingo style, on one foot.

I'm here to heal, Baby reminded herself grimly, wishing she could dive into the river and swim to New Jersey.

"Now, repeat after me. Ahm-ahhh-nom!" Ophelia chanted loudly, letting the m sound hang in the air.

"Um, I've got it," Baby said, really hoping she wouldn't actually have to repeat the syllables out loud. A Circle Line cruise ship passed the park. Ophelia was so loud, Baby was sure the passengers on board heard her. And what *was* that chant, anyway? She'd taken a few yoga classes before, and while they'd done chanting, it never sounded like the elephant-mating-with-a-hippopotamus sounds emanating from Ophelia's mouth.

"I want you to own this word. I want you to chant it seventeen times a day, and I also want you to go on an all-green diet. What we need is for you to detox. I'll help you with that. Together, we can heal!"

She nodded encouragingly. Baby mustered a smile. Maybe it would get better?

Oh, so much better.

o learns the rules

"A little help?" Owen called, his vision obscured by two cardboard boxes full of Speedos. He wasn't sure if he was going to bang into a pile of kickboards or a wooden bench in the guys' locker room. Finally, he dropped the boxes to the wet tiled floor in frustration.

"Get your suits!" he called gruffly. He was still a little annoyed that no one had shown up at Paragon when he'd picked them up yesterday. Eventually, not knowing what else to do, he'd texted Kelsey. She'd met up with him, and they'd hooked up in the dressing rooms by the tennis rackets while one of the shop employees went in search of the St. Jude's suits.

None of the swimmers seemed to notice him. Instead, they were crowded around Hugh Moore. He was wearing a ridiculous pirate-type hat, complete with a feather. Owen's eyes narrowed. Hugh was usually pretty funny, but now wasn't the time. The team really had to come together after their loss last week, and only five practices stood between them and a huge meet with Unity, an Upper East Side boys' school that was one of St. Jude's biggest rivals. If they lost that meet, they were pretty much screwed for the rest of the season.

"Guys?" Owen called again. He climbed onto one of the rickety wooden benches. No one even looked up. They were still clustered around Hugh like he was preaching the gospel.

"Seriously, I'm telling you, if you go to the Barneys lingerie floor, you're *in*, man! All you have to do is pretend you're buying underwear for your girlfriend. I did it once, and a girl totally modeled a teddy for me. Do you guys even know what a teddy is?" Owen overheard Hugh ask the guys.

"Pick up your suits now!" Owen bellowed in frustration.

"Carlyle is trying to say something to you queens." Coach poked his head out from the tiny makeshift office in the corner of the locker room. Owen flushed with embarrassment. Crap. So now Coach knew he didn't even have the guys' attention.

"Got it, Coach!" Hugh yelled back. He leaned in conspiratorially to the huddled team members. "We'll continue this conversation after practice. If you guys are good, I might even take you on a little extra-credit field trip," Hugh said, leading them toward the cardboard box of suits.

"Did you get your suit to say St. Dicks?" Ian McDaniel, a hobbitlike sophomore, asked, glaring at Owen as he pulled a tiny maroon suit from the box. Owen stared at him, mystified. He couldn't even remember *talking* to Ian, much less doing anything to offend him.

"Ha-ha, funny," Owen mumbled, trying to hide his annoyance. "Anyway, guys, I wanted to talk about—"

"Dude, seriously. Skip the speech. I think it's better if we go out and get a kick start on drills before Coach comes out on deck," Hugh interrupted. Owen narrowed his eyes at the broad-shouldered, stubble-faced junior.

"Is there a problem here?" Owen brushed his blond hair from

his eyes and looked out at the swim team members. Ken Williams had his arms crossed angrily over his expansive stomach, and even Chadwick Jenkins, normally a puppyish freshman who worshipped the ground Owen walked on, was staring at him disapprovingly.

"Yup." Hugh took a swig of his blue Gatorade and stared up at Owen. The pirate hat partially obscured his eyes.

Owen wasn't sure if it was the bench or him, but he suddenly felt very shaky. He jumped off the bench and stood, facing Hugh so they were eye to eye.

"I'm going to quote something to you. Are you ready?" Hugh cleared his throat, clearly enjoying the attention. "*Bros before hos.* Learn it and love it, team," Hugh declared, glancing around the group of swimmers. One by one, the members of the team nodded in agreement.

Owen felt his stomach plummet. So that was it—the guys were taking Rhys's side. That's why they hadn't shown up on Sunday. They didn't want to follow Owen. Not to Paragon Sports. Not during practice. Not anywhere.

"And, Owen, let's be clear: It's just a quote, so I'm not making any judgments on your current lady friend," Hugh clarified, grandly stroking his stubbly chin. "But rules are rules. And you broke them. And so, no matter what Coach says, I'm wearing the captain hat. Literally. Thanks for getting this for me, little buddy!" Hugh smiled fondly at Chadwick, tipping his lame pirate hat. Chadwick grinned so widely it looked like his face was going to crack.

"Now that this is settled, let's go practice," Hugh said, taking off his maroon St. Jude's warm-up pants to reveal a St. Dudes Speedo. "Let's go, boys."

Methinks I smell a mutiny. . . .

every good story starts with the truth

"This is stapled wrong," McKenna barked on Tuesday afternoon, disdainfully dropping a pile of editorial calendars on Avery's desk. Since all of the intern desks were currently occupied by college journalism majors, Avery's desk was, in fact, a makeshift table set up next to the vending machines in *Metropolitan*'s alcove kitchen. Luckily, since no one at *Metropolitan* seemed to eat, the area was very quiet. "Fix it," she commanded, glaring disdainfully at the pile as if it were a stack of JCPenney catalogs. Some of the papers fluttered to the floor and underneath the vending machine. McKenna rolled her eyes, as if this was yet another example of Avery's supreme incompetence.

"I'm sorry?" Avery glanced up from a huge pile of business cards she was supposed to organize. She'd raced to *Metropolitan* as soon as school was over, even packing her Marni hobo bag five minutes before the end of AP English. She'd run out of the class as soon as the bell rang, hailed one of the first cabs idling outside the royal blue doors, and gotten to the office a full twenty minutes before she was officially supposed to be on duty. Her plan had been to sneak into Ticky's office before Gemma or McKenna saw her.

It hadn't worked. Gemma had cornered her as soon as she'd walked past the reception desk, and had given her a huge stack of business cards with the assignment to Google all of them and write up reports on her findings. It was so obvious that all the cards were from guys Gemma had either met, hooked up with, or wanted to hook up with, even though she mumbled some explanation about working on a story about guys' grooming habits.

It was so fucking typical. Over the past week, she'd been McKenna and Gemma's personal message girl, sent on missions to return fashion mistakes to Barneys and make coffee runs to Starbucks. Once she'd been forced to go to Duane Reade to pick up McKenna's birth control prescription.

At least we know she's not procreating.

"Gareth, our creative director, has a problem with asymmetry," McKenna sniffed, eyeing Avery accusingly. "He wants staples to either be perpendicular or parallel. No exceptions. Could you fix this? It's important to learn attention to detail." McKenna was wearing a gorgeous brown Prada sweaterdress that had just been worn by Scarlett Johansson on the cover of the October *Elle*. If McKenna hadn't been such a super-bitch, she'd have been pretty, with her flawless skin and so-blond-it-was-almost-white hair.

"I didn't even staple those," Avery stated matter-of-factly. Didn't McKenna realize that copier duty would be a step up from what she was doing now?

"I don't have time to hear about what you did or did not do," McKenna said, primly. "Restaple them, then bring them to the editorial meeting in the conference room in ten minutes. Do you think you can handle that, Intern?" McKenna stomped off, glancing disparagingly at the vending machine, as if Avery had single-handedly dragged it in herself, just to be annoying. *Well, fine.* Avery took a staple remover and savagely stabbed at the offensively asymmetrical staples with it.

Once she was done, her fingers looking like they'd been chewed by baby piranhas, Avery hurriedly shoved the papers into a pile and rushed down the hall to the glass-enclosed conference room. As soon as she saw a few top-level editors huddled over multicolored layouts on the sleek glass conference table, her heart began to thump wildly in her chest. Maybe the stapling assignment wasn't so crappy after all.

"Here you go." Avery smiled a slow, *let's all be friends* smile around the room and began passing out the calendars to the editors around the table. No one looked up.

"Cheers! Are you a new hire?" A guy with sparkling blue eyes and a Scottish accent smiled as Avery set the sheaf of papers down next to him. He wore a pair of perfectly faded Diesel jeans and a blue wool vest over a checked button-down shirt in an off-duty-rock-star-meets-professor look. On most people, it would look totally dorky, but on this guy it looked intellectual, especially with his light stubble and square jaw. He was actually kind of cute. More than kind of.

Avery smiled broadly. "I'm Avery Carlyle, an—"

"She's the intern," McKenna interrupted, snatching the papers from Avery's hand. "So sorry, James," McKenna hissed as she ushered Avery to the door. "I'll deal with you later." McKenna glanced at her white gold Rolex watch. "Shit, I've got to get Ticky!" she exclaimed, flying out of the room and leaving the editorial calendars in a pile on the edge of the conference room table.

"I can see they're giving you the glamorous work," James called over. Avery smiled back, unsure whether or not he was making fun of her. She edged toward the back of the conference room, where the associate-level editors were sitting on the floor, obviously not senior enough for the privilege of sitting in the Eames chairs surrounding the conference room table. Surely no one would notice her back here? She settled in a corner next to a giant half-dead potted palm, drawing her knees up to her chest to make herself fit.

Suddenly, all the editors' heads snapped toward the door of the conference room. Ticky walked in, leaning heavily on McKenna for support, unbalanced on her five-inch, rainbow-colored, sequin-bedazzled pumps. She wore a black St. John power suit, and had five Cartier diamond necklaces wrapped around her skinny neck. Her henna-dyed hair was teased into a reddish bouffant above her widow's peak.

Avery sucked in her breath as Ticky tottered past, unsure whether she should pipe up and say hi or remain incognito. She remembered what Baby said about laying low and chose the latter, leaning even closer into the potted palm.

"McKenna, can you be a doll and pick up my sparkles?" Avery overheard Ticky whisper loudly into McKenna's ear. Dutifully, McKenna got on her hands and knees and started to pick up the tiny sequins that had fallen off Ticky's shoes. For a brief moment, Avery was worried that McKenna would see her, but she was too busy scanning the tacky blue industrial carpet. Avery felt a tiny stab of sympathy when she saw McKenna's couture-clad knees on the floor. It had to suck to spend your workday picking up after your boss.

Says the girl who color-codes lip stains.

"Well, my pets, impress me," Ticky rasped as she settled into the black leather chair at the head of the conference room table.

She folded her hands in front of her and looked around the table expectantly, her eyebrows raised high on her heavily Botoxed forehead. McKenna rushed toward Ticky to deposit a small pile of sequins by her side, then took the seat of honor to the left of Ticky's chair.

"Well, we had the idea about drunkorexia. It's like, the new edgy disorder that combines anorexia and alcoholism. Everyone's talking about it," Gemma began knowledgeably. "But, what I was thinking is going undercover at Rose Bar and just recording how many drinks girls get and whether or not they order food. We could compare that to men. I think that'd be sort of a scientific way to approach the story," Gemma began hopefully. From her pale skin, shaky hands, and super-skinny frame, Avery had no doubt Gemma was a drunkorexic herself.

"Or the idea about ex-mates. You know, the people who live together even though they're so totally over, for real estate?" another assistant suggested hopefully as she pushed a sheaf of papers toward Ticky. She wore American Apparel leggings and a purple Betsey Johnson wool tunic dress that barely covered her ass. Although her look was obviously a tribute to Edie Sedgwick, it pretty much looked like she'd forgotten her pants.

"Drunkorexia and ex-mates." Ticky laughed bitterly to herself. "Is this your college paper? Is this the 'I don't give a fuck' news? Everyone's a goddamn drunkorexic in this town. I *invented* drunkorexia. It's not news. It's not *Metropolitan*." Ticky angrily pushed herself out of the chair. McKenna practically toppled *her* chair over to stand and support her, while the other editors pretended to be preoccupied by the editorial calendars on the table.

"No. We need glamour," Ticky intoned, stopping two feet in

front of Avery to address the table. "Intrigue. To remind people that Manhattan still matters. *Manhattan.* Not Brooklyn or Queens or goddamn Philadelphia. *Metropolitan* readers live on islands. Remember that," Ticky lectured. She sounded angry, but Avery thought she could detect a vague sense of wistfulness. Avery could understand. She'd grown up on her grandmother's photo albums and stories. Ever since she moved here, she'd found herself looking for a New York that didn't seem to exist: one filled with gracious socialites, a never-ending stream of invitations, and a bevy of male suitors just waiting to whisk her off her feet.

Was she also looking for a time machine to take her back to 1897?

"Well, what about that Cashman Lofts campaign? The girl who's on the posters—Jacqueline Laurent? She's something like sixteen, but she's out every night and of course, she's gorgeous. The next Tinsley Mortimer," Alex Abramson, the tall, model-esque, Prada-clad executive editor finally suggested. Avery recognized her from her Ask Alex column. Although it was a totally lame column name, the actual feature was snarky and smart, filled with random advice on everything from how to eat oysters without looking obscene to how to get rid of a social climber who's obviously using you for your NetJet connection. Alex coolly raised a perfectly groomed blond eyebrow at Ticky, as if daring her to say no.

"She hasn't gotten much exposure yet, and I think we could break a story on her. She's from New York, has a wealthy father and a former-dancer mother, her boyfriend is Dick Cashman's son—think of all the angles," Alex continued smoothly.

Avery snuck a glance over at Ticky, hoping she'd be shaking her head or rolling her eyes. But no. Ticky was on the edge of her seat, her brown eyes shining in excitement. Avery wanted to scream in frustration. She was tempted to stand up and stomp back to the beauty closet, just so she wouldn't have to listen to more Jack Laurent worship.

"Isn't she a bit young?" Ticky finally asked.

Yes, yes, yes! Avery wanted to scream as several of the editors laughed politely.

"Oh, but she's lovely. Classic beauty. She doesn't look like a celebutard at all," Cheryl Katz, the red-haired beauty director, piped up from another end of the table, dashing Avery's hopes.

A flamboyant man wearing a checkered bow tie, ass-tight black jodhpurs that reached his knee, and a crisp short-sleeve white shirt practically jumped off his chair in excitement.

"Yes, Yves?" Ticky asked, pursing her lips as she nodded to him.

"Think about it, darling! We'd have so many options for shooting. We could do some sort of Old New York glamour thing of her in her town house, then juxtapose it with her against an ultramodern, eco-chic backdrop at the lofts. The possibilities are endless."

Avery laughed quietly to herself. Now she wanted them to do the story. She couldn't wait for Yves and the rest of the *Metropolitan* staff to see the crumbling plaster ceiling and rickety staircase that were all part of the tacky walk-up garret Jack lived in with her mom.

Suddenly, Avery noticed all eyes were curiously looking down at her.

"Yes?" Yves asked, sounding pissed. Uh-oh. Avery hadn't realized she'd laughed out loud.

"Sorry!" she exclaimed, scooting away from the potted plant

only to find her hair tangled in one of the half-dead leaves. "I mean, I just know Jack Laurent, and her life's not really like that," she explained, finally yanking her blond strands free.

"How do you know her?" Alex asked curiously, gazing down at Avery with her cool blue eyes. "And, forgive me, but *who* are you?"

"Sorry. Um. Yes. I'm an intern," Avery explained. "My name's Avery Carlyle. I've been mostly in the closet. I mean, the beauty closet! I mean, I'm just learning a lot," Avery babbled.

So much for old-fashioned poise.

"Avery Carlyle!" Ticky exclaimed delightedly, tottering over to Avery's corner and reaching her spindly arm down to help Avery stand up. Avery quickly pulled herself to her feet, not wanting to be responsible for breaking Ticky's frail arm.

With her luck . . .

"Hi Ticky," Avery greeted her awkwardly, aware that all eyes were on them.

"I've been passing-out *busy* these past few days, but you'd think someone would tell me you were here!" Ticky glared at the editors around the table. "You have to forgive me—and these morons. We've all been killing ourselves getting the past beast of an issue out the door—I haven't even had time to *smoke*.

"McKenna, move," Ticky announced flatly. "Avery, darling, sit next to me." McKenna flashed her McBitchiest smile at Avery as she scooted out of the chair. Avery cautiously hovered near the table, unsure what to do.

"Avery, sit," Ticky commanded.

Good girl!

"Now then, the glamour girls of Manhattan," Ticky mused thoughtfully. "See, that's a *Metropolitan* story. That's why I have

Alex and Yves on the payroll. The question is, why do I bother with the rest of you?" Ticky shook her head sadly. "Avery, since you're in Jack Laurent's world, you're on the story with James. He's my best reporter. We'll crash it into next week's issue." She clapped her hands together. "I'm so glad *some* people around here have ideas. Meeting dismissed."

Avery locked eyes with James, the cute reporter who'd made fun of her intern status earlier.

"You don't say no to Ticky." James winked one of his blue eyes at Avery. "Let's meet on Wednesday to discuss?" he asked across the table so everyone could hear. Avery nodded giddily.

It's a date!

meanwhile, back at the lofts

"Hello?" Jack yelled as she opened the door to her penthouse apartment Monday night. She'd just come from an afternoon ballet class across town, and she was sweaty, exhausted, and hungry. She was hoping J.P. was still at squash practice so she could take a long, hot shower, change into something sexy, and meet him at the door with a drink.

"Hey, gorgeous, I missed you!"

Jack smiled tightly. Sitting in the middle of the newspaper-strewn floor was J.P., clad in a pair of black Riverside Prep track pants and his dorky yellow Riverside Prep Squash polo shirt. The dog was yapping and jumping around him excitedly.

"Look, she can fetch!" J.P. exclaimed, taking a red rubber bone and throwing it toward Jack. It hit her hard in the knee.

"Great," Jack said faintly. Couldn't he *forget* about the dog for a second? It had been like that last night, too. Every time they left it in its organic cotton doggie bed in the kitchen, the puppy would start whining until finally they had to wedge it between them in bed to get it to fall asleep.

"I named her, too," J.P. announced, picking up the dog and

walking over to Jack. "I thought Magellan might be cute, even if she is a girl. Just because she's so good at discovering things." J.P. held up a pair of chewed-up black velvet Tory Burch flats like a trophy. "She found your shoes. She had to dig way into the closet to get them, too," he added proudly.

"What the *fuck*?" Jack asked, snatching the shoes away. Thank goodness they were ancient. Still, the dog had fucking *eaten* her shoes and J.P. was rewarding it with a lame name?

"She didn't know any better!" J.P. exclaimed, scooping up the puppy. He held out its paw, making it wave at Jack. "She says she's sorry. Anyway, you know how my dad likes naming our dogs after explorers." He shrugged. It was true. For some reason, Dick Cashman's dogs—Nemo, Shackleton and Darwin—were all named after real or imaginary explorers, a fact he'd readily tell anyone who asked. "Are you and Magellan friends again?"

"Where are we going to dinner?" Jack asked, changing the subject. Her ballet class had been intense, and she was *starving*. "Maybe Gramercy Tavern?" she suggested. She couldn't wait to share a bottle of wine, eat a huge steak, and cuddle in a cozy leather booth while other couples eyed them jealously.

"Oh." J.P. frowned and placed Magellan near Jack's feet. The dog let out a low-pitched whine and ran away from Jack. "I thought we could make dinner tonight. You know, to christen our kitchen."

"Fine," Jack sighed, trying to rein in her frustration. That was *not* the type of christening Jack had had in mind, but in a way, it was kind of sweet that J.P. loved being so domestic. Her mom was a histrionic French dancer who had subsisted on eight hundred calories a day for the past two decades, so Jack had learned how to order in by the time she was eight. Why *make* food if so many people were willing to do it for you?

"I printed out some recipes," J.P. continued, pulling a sheaf of papers from the counter and handing them to her: *lamb tagine, goat cheese bread pudding* . . . Jack continued to riffle through the Epicurious.com printouts, a smile slowly curling her lips. They could actually *make* all this stuff? The recipes sounded like food she'd actually order.

"We can really do this?" Jack asked, glancing from the recipes up to J.P.'s face. She suddenly revised her evening fantasy. Instead, they'd be huddled together by the counter, their hips touching. J.P. would reach over her shoulder to add a dash of whatever spice you cooked with and then suddenly, he'd press her against the counter and . . .

"Sure," J.P. replied confidently.

A little too confidently?

He began rummaging through the Sub-Zero refrigerator, pulling various ingredients out. Jack spotted several unopened bottles of organic wine on the counter, clearly another house-warming present. She eagerly picked one up, pulled a corkscrew from a drawer, and plunged it into the bottle.

"Wine?" she asked sweetly.

J.P. nodded absently, his brow furrowed in consternation as he squinted at the recipe. He dislodged ingredients from the cupboards, throwing them into the bright orange Le Creuset pot sitting on the six-burner range. He alternately mixed and added, every so often consulting the recipe like it held the secrets to life.

Jack tried to conceal her boredom. "Come over *here*," she needled, setting the two glasses of wine at the opposite end of the counter. What was the point of preparing a romantic dinner if there was no *romance* involved?

"One *second*," J.P. said, a little brusquely. "I mean, let me just finish," he amended. Jack sulkily drained her glass of wine, then refilled it.

Finally, J.P. stopped whatever he was doing and sat down next to her. Jack realized she'd already downed her second glass of wine.

"So, we're all alone . . ." Jack began, rubbing his ankle with her foot.

"Aren't you glad we stayed in?" J.P. asked huskily. He leaned toward Jack, and she could smell his familiar, delicious scent of eucalyptus.

"Yes," Jack said, kissing him. Suddenly, she forgot all her annoyances.

Just then Jack heard a splashing sound. She pulled away and glanced toward the stove. The pot was bubbling over, sending cascades of water onto the floor.

Magellan emitted a low-pitched whine, then crouched and began peeing on the floor, as if to add to the flood.

"Shit!" J.P. said as he hurried toward the stove and quickly turned off the burner. A faint burning smell hung in the air. He grabbed a roll of recycled paper towels and threw them on the floor. The scratchy brown paper slowly absorbed all the water. Next, J.P. moved over to the small puddle Magellan had left, adjacent to the counter. Jack looked away, not wanting to watch as her handsome boyfriend knelt to mop up dog pee.

When he was finished cleaning, J.P. offered a small smile. "You want to choose the recipe this time?"

"Let's just order," Jack sighed, completely forgetting about their kiss just a moment ago.

"Okay. You pick somewhere and I'll take the dog for a walk." J.P. was already clipping the Louis Vuitton leash around Magellan's Swarovski crystal–bedecked collar, another gift courtesy of Tatyana.

"Sure," Jack said, not even saying goodbye as she took another swig of her wine. She picked up a menu for a gross diner nearby. Right now, all she wanted was a greasy grilled cheese and fries, and she wanted them fast. She was happy to have the apartment to herself for a little bit.

And who said there was never such a thing as being *too* close?

gossipgirl.net

Disclaimer: All the real names of places, people, and events have been altered or abbreviated to protect the innocent. Namely, me.

topics	sightings	your e-mail	post a question

hey people!

We've been doing it since our very first day in preschool at All Souls on Lexington, and now that we're older, it's the one game we still play. I'm talking about playing house, and once the houses are real, it gets *really* interesting. Whether it's a sprawling cottage on Sea Island, a pied-à-terre on Madison, or a villa in Tuscany, one rule remains the same: With great real estate comes great responsibility. Especially when it comes to throwing a housewarming party, like the one planned for this Friday night at the Cashman Lofts—the building's big unveiling. Here are some helpful housekeeping hints to keep in mind, for the next time you want to plan a party:

Designate rooms. Creating a solid floor plan is key. No party is oomplete without a VIP room, so make sure to put the good booze in a special place, for your special guests—leave the Cosmos for the girls who were lucky just to score an invite. Most importantly, lock the master bedroom. Left unguarded, someone is guaranteed to have sex on your parents' thousand-thread-count silk sheets, or throw up on the antique Turkish rug.

Institute a tough door policy. If your home is your castle, it's up to you to choose your court. Let your doorman know who can come in and who can't—he'll be happy to play bouncer for the night.

Make it look easy. The goal of any party is to make your guests think this is how you live all the time. First, scan the house with a critical eye.

Hide all evidence of your childhood and your parents' weird hobbies (that means the nutcracker collection has to go). Hire a cleaning service for both before *and* after the party, but make sure the place still feels lived-in, otherwise you'll look totally OCD.

And most important of all: While the people you've so wisely hired are prepping the place, **make yourself look great**. After all, *you're* the centerpiece!

your e-mail

q:

Hey girl!
When and where exactly is the party?
—buzzbuzz

a:

Dear Buzz,
If you don't know, then you probably weren't invited. Sorry!
—GG

q:

Dear Gossip Girl,
I work for this really cool fashion mag, and now we have an intern who's getting all the credit for, like, major feature stories. Our editor so obvi loves her, which is super unfortch for the rest of us. It's not like I'm jealy or anything, but she's, like, eight years old. WTF?
—madddd

a:

Dear M,
Sounds like there might indeed be a case of, um, jealy-ness going on. Regardless of the intern's age, have you ever thought she just may have a better grasp of the English language than you?
—GG

sightings

B and some crazy-haired lady at a natural foods store in the village, stocking up on essential oils and bottles of green stuff that resembles mulch. Taking the green movement a little *too* literally? . . . **O** sucking **K**'s lips off near the Romeo and Juliet statue in Central Park. Symbolic, or convenient? . . . **J** and her sometimes besties, **S.J.**, the other **J**, and **G**, in the VIP rooms of parties at **Bungalow**, the **Eldridge**, and **Beatrice**—all in the same night. It pays to have friends—or boyfriends—in high places! . . . **A** and her new mentor, Ticky Bensimmon-Heart, heading toward Ticky's chauffeured Mercedes S-Class waiting outside the Dennen building. Looks like **A**'s acing her crash course in office politics. . . . **R** sitting with a Hacky Sack on a bench by the East Lawn, looking dejected, then heading home. Sad!

one more note

Now it's time for a housekeeping rule of my own: No matter how fabulous my surroundings, it's always my goal to make *me* more fabulous. So with that in mind, I'm heading to Cornelia Day Resort for an oxygen clarifying masque and a honey citrus body polish. Remember: A little cleanup goes a long way!

You know you love me,

healing is where the heart is

The sun was high over the park at noon on Tuesday, but Baby couldn't stop shivering. She pulled her baggy red Nantucket High sweatshirt closer around her skinny frame and leaned against the stone wall of Engineers Gate, the official entrance to the Central Park Reservoir. She'd been following Ophelia's regimen of essential oil application and juice fasting, which meant she could only drink premade green smoothies of juiced lettuce, cucumbers, and apples. But instead of feeling energized and in control, she felt greasy, hungry, and tired.

And crazier than ever?

Mustering up her energy, Baby shuffled up the steps leading to the reservoir and stepped onto the pebble-covered surface of the running trail. Ugh. She felt dizzy.

"Babs! Hold on a sec!" Coach Mann, the unfortunately named female gym teacher, sprinted up the steps after her. She grabbed Baby's long, tangled brown hair in an attempt to stop her from taking off.

"Ow!" Baby rubbed her head.

"I didn't hurt you, Babs," Coach countered calmly. "You

aren't running today. Come with me," she said, marching Baby back down the steps while twirling her pink, smiley face sticker–covered whistle in a figure-eight pattern.

"Yes, sir!" Baby whispered under her breath. Ever since school had started, Coach Mann had insisted on calling her Babs, which made her feel like some fifty-nine-year-old gum-smacking waitress from Oklahoma. She obediently followed Coach to a shady spot under an elm tree.

"I heard that Baby has, like, this really weird communicable disease. That's why she's only been drinking green juice. It's because she's not allowed to touch anything in the cafeteria," Baby overheard Jiffy Bennett whisper to Chelsy Chapin, a small, pug-nosed sophomore.

Baby glowered. It was so unfair! There was so much psychological warfare going on amongst all these bitchy girls, and *she* was the one Mrs. McLean recommended for therapy.

"Babs, I'm worried about you," Coach barked, as if expressly for the listening pleasure of the gaggle of tenth graders huddled by the water fountain, not even pretending to stretch. "You haven't looked so good recently. Are you in some sort of trouble? You can talk to me," Coach added generously, as if Baby would really spill her deepest darkest secrets to Coach Mann. She had a salt-and-pepper mullet, and sort of looked like Mel Gibson, except for her humongous boobs.

"Is it drugs?" Coach Mann asked, narrowing her eyes into even smaller slits, obviously enjoying the interrogation process. "I want to help you, Babs."

"Thanks," Baby hedged. Everything suddenly seemed far too complicated to explain, and Baby was too tired. "I think I need to go to the nurse," she lied, running out of the park. She glanced behind her, half expecting to see Coach Mann chasing after her. Instead, there were just a few nannies pushing strollers, a guy running his golden Lab, and squirrels jumping in and out of the bushes. Baby sighed. Maybe she really *should* go to the nurse, she realized as she stood on the corner, waiting for the WALK sign on the other side of Eighty-sixth Street. She felt weird, like her brain wasn't completely connected to her body.

"Baby!"

She squinted to see Sydney on the other side of the crosswalk. She wore knee-high boots and a red peace sign T-shirt under her Constance blazer, and she carried oversize stereo headphones attached to her silver iPod nano. She looked like she was on her way to DJ at an underground Williamsburg club.

"Double photog?" Baby called, glancing at the digital camera swinging from Sydney's wrist.

Sydney crossed her eyes. "That's what Mr. Beckham would like to think. I actually went to hang out with Webber uptown," Sydney answered. Her boyfriend was a sophomore at Columbia. Baby had hung out with him and his friends when she and Sydney were working on *Rancor* last month.

"I love how we only see each other when we're ditching school. Great minds think alike!" Sydney yelled. She didn't seem to care that pedestrians could hear every word she was calling across the crosswalk. Baby smiled, feeling more energized than she had all day. She loved hanging out with Sydney, who simply didn't give a fuck.

The sign changed to WALK, and Baby followed the hordes of tourists across the street.

"Picture!" Sydney called as they met in the middle, holding out the camera and snapping a picture of Baby. Sydney pulled it back and frowned at the small screen. "God, you look like hell," she remarked.

"Get out of the way!" A cab beeped and Baby realized they were still standing in the middle of the crosswalk.

"Fuck you!" Sydney yelled as she took the crook of Baby's elbow and ran her across the street.

"What's wrong?" Sydney's heavily lined eyes narrowed sharply, as if she'd just noticed something was seriously amiss with Baby. "Are you using some of your sister's beauty products? Because they totally don't work on you. Your face is really oily," Sydney remarked matter-of-factly. She stuck her index finger on Baby's cheek, then held it in front of Baby's face triumphantly. Even Baby was a little grossed out at the shininess of Sydney's finger.

"Thanks," Baby replied sarcastically. She was so not in the mood for this.

"Dude, what's up with the bitch vibe?" Sydney remarked calmly. "Are you okay? And why aren't *you* in class? You're a bad influence." She smirked.

"No, I just ran out," Baby explained. She giggled. It *was* sort of funny, when she thought about it.

"You made a run for it during gym? I love it! You're such a rebel. Remind me why you haven't been kicked out yet?" Sydney smiled, clearly teasing.

Baby looked into Sydney's large, expressive eyes and suddenly wanted to explain everything to her. "I'm *going* to get kicked out if I don't finish my therapy sessions," she said, close to tears. "I just don't know what to do!" she added in a rush of words.

"Oh my God. You need to come with me. You need to take a

shower, you need to eat, and you need to just chill the fuck out," Sydney said kindly. She stuck out her hand and expertly hailed a cab sailing down Fifth Avenue.

"Ninety-third and West End," Sydney announced without taking an eye off Baby. Then, Sydney stuck her nose up in the air and inhaled deeply. "Do you have air freshener?" She stuck her head through the Plexiglas partition of the cab. The cabbie nodded wordlessly and passed an aerosol spray can back to her.

"No offense," Sydney remarked. Baby shook her head. Honestly, now that they were in a closed space, she could sort of smell the essential oils on herself.

"Give me that!" Baby wrestled the aerosol container away from Sydney and sprayed it liberally on herself.

"Here's where I live. Welcome to the Upper West Side," Sydney said as the cab stopped in front of a crumbling but distinguished-looking redbrick building. "My mom's a therapist and my dad writes a column on manners for the Style section of the *New York Times*, but he lives in DC. It's the only way their marriage works." Sydney smirked and escorted Baby into the old-fashioned cage elevator and pressed five.

"This is nice," Baby exclaimed as Sydney flung open the door to a bright and airy apartment. Unlike the apartments she'd seen on the Upper East Side, which reminded her of museum exhibits with their Louis XIV–style furniture, Sydney's apartment looked lived-in and comfortable. Floor-to-ceiling bookshelves flanked the hallways, holding first editions and galleys of books, and the walls were covered with art.

"You. Shower." Sydney pointed inside the large old-fashioned bathroom. A claw-footed tub stood in the center of the room. Sydney marched onto the black and white tiled floor and turned on the water. Quickly, steam filled up the room. "Promise you won't faint?" Sydney commanded. Baby shook her head and closed the door.

Finally, Baby emerged from the bathroom. Sydney had thoughtfully left clothes folded on a wicker hamper, so Baby wore a ripped Lollapalooza '93 T-shirt and a loose black American Apparel skirt. She felt more like herself than she had the past few days.

"So much better," Sydney cried in relief once Baby wandered into the cheerful blue-and-white kitchen. "I *definitely* earned my gold star with you for today. You were a mess."

"That's what happens when I don't eat. Food?" Baby asked hopefully, glancing at the pine cabinets. The kitchen reminded Baby of their Nantucket home. Instead of feeling a pang of homesickness, though, she felt relaxed.

"Here you go." Sydney nodded matter-of-factly at a goat cheese and arugula salad sitting on the counter

"You made that?" Baby asked in disbelief. Sydney was full of surprises.

Besides her inappropriate piercings?

"Yeah, I just put on my wifey apron and whipped up lunch. No, you dumbass, I ordered!" Sydney rolled her large brown eyes as she plucked a cherry tomato from the top of Baby's salad, popped it in her mouth, and sat down. She chewed thoughtfully. "I didn't know what you wanted, so I just got a whole lot of crap." Sydney shrugged and motioned toward two more takeout containers. "Do you feel better? And why the fuck were you on a starvation diet? Was it because Mrs. McLean's on vacation this week and you were pining for her?"

"No," Baby shot back. "I was doing this detox thing. My new therapist recommended it."

"That's lame," Sydney said, pushing one of the takeout containers over to Baby. She took the lid off. "Grilled cheese?"

Baby nodded gratefully. "What's this?" She eyed a book on the counter called *Your Life Isn't That Complicated*. She raised an eyebrow. Really? Because it certainly seemed that way. She picked it up and thumbed through the earmarked pages.

"Oh, my mom's book." Sydney rolled her eyes. "Basically, her whole philosophy is that people need to clean their closets, throw shit out, and they'll be happier. She charges five hundred dollars an hour to tell people this. Not like it does much good. Whenever she gets in a fight with my dad, she gets over it by hauling crap down to the Goodwill on the corner. I've had to buy so much of my stuff back from there," Sydney added darkly.

"Can I borrow it?" Baby asked hopefully. On the back was a picture of Sydney's mom. She looked a few years older than Baby's own mom, had dark brown hair cut into a neat bob around her smiling, angular face. She looked nice and no-nonsense.

"Sure. I guess you can't get any more fucked up than you already are," Sydney hedged suspiciously.

"Are you sure about that?" Baby asked, teasingly. Maybe it was just the promise of food, but she suddenly felt like a great weight had been lifted from her shoulders. Baby grabbed a sandwich out of one of the takeout boxes and took a bite, loving the taste of the gooey cheese as it hit the roof of her mouth.

"Nah, you're pretty fucked up," Sydney said, laughing. "Here's to adolescent rebellion. Highly underrated." Sydney arched her eyebrow.

Hear, hear!

r's magical mystery tour

Rhys slid his new iPhone out of the pocket of his khaki pants as Mr. Schorr, his AP English teacher, droned on about John Donne. Everyone called him Mr. Snore and used the class period to catch up on texts or homework for other classes. Mr. Schorr didn't seem to mind. One time, he'd put *himself* to sleep while reading aloud from *The Iliad*, only sputtering back to attention once his head hit the wooden desk.

Rhys made sure Mr. Schorr's back was turned to him, then looked back down at his phone's tiny display.

Dude, U okay? Want to go watch a L'École volleyball game tonight? U need to get laid. I heard they don't wear sports bras. . . .

Rhys looked back and saw Hugh, grinning broadly and giving him the thumbs-up sign. Rhys shook his head. Even bra-less French girls playing a sport that involved lots of jumping couldn't excite him.

He looked up to see Mr. Schorr lumbering toward him. Uh-oh. "'Batter my heart, three person'd God!'" Mr. Schorr wildly pounded the wooden desk in front of Rhys, spraying droplets of spit on the polished surface.

"Sir?" Rhys straightened in his chair, not even bothering to hide his phone. What the fuck was the point?

"May I pull you away from your own matters of the flesh to invite you to take a break with me and Mr. John Donne?" Mr. Schorr asked sarcastically.

"I'm sorry, sir," Rhys mumbled. Mr. Schorr was still standing at his desk, tapping his foot theatrically for the benefit of the rest of the class.

"May I also remind you, Mr. Sterling, that we haven't quite yet hit the iPhone era of literature." He laughed at his dorky joke. "As such, I'll take that for now." Mr. Schorr held out his palm. Several other kids in the back of the class groaned. While phones weren't officially allowed in school, every other teacher just turned a blind eye to the texting going on in class.

"Mister Sterling?" Mr. Schorr prompted again. Rhys sighed and slapped the phone into Mr. Schorr's hand. Then he stood up, his wooden chair clattering to the dark blue and white carpet with a muffled thud.

"I'm out of here. Keep the phone," Rhys muttered as he slung his distressed-leather Tumi bag over one St. Jude's blazer–clad shoulder and walked out the door.

Talk about poetic!

He quickly marched down the hallway, down the stairs, and outside to East End Avenue. His heart was thudding in his chest. He'd never walked out of class before.

He aimlessly wandered toward the park, not caring about the DON'T WALK sign or the two girls with Constance skirts running across the street. The taller girl smirked at him as she passed, clearly acknowledging him as a partner in crime, before she and her friend got into a taxi. But while that girl looked happy and free, Rhys felt miserable. He couldn't believe he'd given his fucking phone to his English teacher.

He walked south, past the groups of tourists enjoying the fall sunshine on the steps of the Met, past the Frick museum, until he got to East Lawn, where he'd seen those hippies playing Hacky Sack a few days before. The lawn was mostly filled with kids and their nannies. He sat on a bench, next to a lady throwing crumbs to pigeons.

"Hey bro!"

Rhys looked up, shielding his eyes from the sun. He saw the hippie from the other day jogging toward him, carrying a big green JanSport backpack. He was wearing the same yellow shirt as before, but the cords had been replaced with a pair of filthy green shorts. His blond dreadlocks were haphazardly pulled into a bun on the top of his head. "I knew you'd be here!"

Rhys nodded. *How?*

Stoner-sense?

The hippie made his way over, trailed by a few of his fellow Hacky Sackers. "What's your name? I'm Lucas," the guy said, "and these are my buddies, Vince, Lisa, and Malia." He pointed to the people gathered behind him.

"Hey." Rhys looked from one guy whose jeans were belted with a frayed rope to a girl with two braids hanging on either side of her head to a tiny girl with short, spiky hair in a bandanna and a lip ring. "Rhys," he finally said.

"So, man, I've got some herb if you want. Or are you good?" Lucas sat down next to Rhys and held out a joint in his hand. Rhys took it without thinking, awkwardly pinching it between his fingers. Was he supposed to just drag from it? Light it? He had no idea what to do.

"Why are you here?" Rhys asked, nonsensically. He realized he was holding the joint the way he'd hold one of his dad's H. Upmann cigars. His dad always brought them out during sweeps week for *Tea with Lady Sterling.*

Close by, Lisa and Malia were arranging a faded tie-dye tapestry on the lawn under a large oak tree. It was obvious that Lisa wasn't wearing a bra under her threadbare patchwork dress. Once they were settled, Lisa pulled a ukulele out of a case and began awkwardly playing the first few notes of "Norwegian Wood," while Malia sighed in contentment, resting her head on Lisa's lap. Rhys looked on in amazement. They weren't hot or pretty at all, but they just seemed so comfortable and at peace with themselves, he couldn't tear his eyes away.

"Don't you have school or something?" Rhys asked again, still passing the joint from one hand to the other, trying to decide if he wanted to smoke it.

"Dude, this is our park." Lucas shrugged mysteriously. He took the joint back from Rhys, lit it with a Zippo lighter, and took a deep hit, as if he could sense Rhys needed a demonstration. "Go for it," Lucas offered, passing it back. Rhys awkwardly placed the joint between his lips and took a deep breath, trying not to cough as he held the smoke inside his lungs. Finally he exhaled, sputtering.

"First times are rough," Lucas said understandingly.

"How did you know?" Rhys asked in wonderment. He wasn't sure if it was the pot or just the fact that Lucas and his friends were completely different from anyone he'd known, but he was starting to feel . . . loose. Like his life didn't suck that bad. Like maybe all there was to life was enjoying the sunshine and the pigeons in Central Park on a warm fall day.

You just keep telling yourself that.

"I just know." Lucas shrugged and held up his hand to shield his eyes from the sun. Rhys noticed there were pink flecks of nail polish on his otherwise dirt-encrusted fingernails. "Come hang for a while," he offered grandly, gesturing to the blanket where Vince, Malia, and Lisa had set up camp. Malia was now braiding dandelions into Vince's dirty brown hair. Rhys and Lucas sat down on the tapestry. "We just came from Citarella, so we have snacks!" Lucas spread out his arms above the blanket.

Rhys looked skeptically at the motley collection of bread and vegetables spread on the grass. Citarella was a gourmet grocery store his mother loved. This food looked like it had been found in a Dumpster.

"Afternoons are good since it's slow. They go through inventory," Lucas said mysteriously, as he offered a bruised eggplant to Rhys. It looked like it had been involved in a game of catch. Rhys shook his head.

"No?" Lucas looked disappointed. "You want an orange?" He threw a greenish one over to Rhys. "Next time you'll have to stake out the selection with us. 'Cause right now, dude, you're being the *ultimate* freegan." Lucas laughed and bit into the raw eggplant. It made a weird crunching sound.

"Oh, no. I eat meat," Rhys contradicted. One time when he was eleven his mom had made him accompany her to a raw food restaurant and it had tasted so gross he'd thrown up for the rest of the day. "Good British stock!" his dad had said, as if he was proud of Rhys for not being able to stomach an organic, raw food diet.

"Yeah, dude." Lucas nodded. "We do, too. We're *freegans*," he said slowly, as if that explained it. "We only eat food that's free.

It used to be called Dumpster diving, but that's a condescending term obviously springing from a deep capitalistic sort of snobbery." Lucas nodded, then took another bite of eggplant.

Rhys wrinkled his nose through his pot-induced haze. Was Lucas for real? Were they really getting food from *Dumpsters*? He should step up and offer to help them. It'd be a sort of charity. He could write his college essay on it, then maybe get a Nobel Prize for his humanitarianism.

"I have food at my house, and I live a few blocks away. You're welcome to stop by anytime," Rhys offered gallantly. He just hoped they'd take showers beforehand.

"Oh, that's all right, my friend. I live right over there." Lucas pointed over the tops of the trees to one of the high-rise luxury buildings flanking Fifth Avenue. "We're just doing our part to not consume. But no pressure. We accept everyone here. Sit down." Lucas smiled.

"Think about it. Eggplant." Lucas addressed the group. "Like, who thought of that?" He stroked the rubbery-looking skin of the vegetable in wonder. Rhys nodded. Suddenly, the bulbous vegetable *did* seem a little bit ridiculous.

"Yeah, because it's not an egg and it's not really a plant." Lisa giggled. "It should be called, like, a purple walrus!"

Rhys laughed. "Hey bro, have a light?" he asked awkwardly. Vince leaned forward with his lighter. He wasn't sure if he was supposed to hold it or breathe out or . . . *fuck*. Suddenly, he burst into a sputtering cough, spewing droplets of spit all over the eggplant.

"Yeah, man, good toke." Vince smiled thoughtfully, in a pot-induced haze. Rhys smiled, dragging more smoke into his lungs.

"Do you do this every day?" Rhys asked in wonderment, gazing at his new friends' sunny, happy faces.

And where can he sign up?

"You wanna know?" Lucas rolled onto his elbow and whispered into Rhys's ear. "We're on our walkabout."

"What?" Walkabout? Was that some type of workout? College course?

"It's like, we all go to Darrow, and we have this whole semester to just discover ourselves. Some people went to Africa, some people are building houses in Central America, but we just decided to stay and experience ourselves. It's actually pretty trippy. What's your story?" Lucas asked, taking another huge hit.

Rhys nodded slowly. Darrow was a school in the village where kindergartners were taught in the same classes as seniors. All the Upper East Side schools made fun of the school's abysmal college admissions record, where only one senior had gotten into an Ivy in the past five years. But now, Rhys suddenly felt a wave of annoyance at himself that he'd ever made fun of the school. After all, *why* care about grades and sports and being the best? Why did it matter?

"I'm on a walkabout too," Rhys announced. Starting now.

"Cool, man!" Lucas said easily.

Rhys leaned back again and gazed up at the puffy, cotton candy–textured clouds, suddenly feeling ridiculously content.

underwear shopping is not a spectator sport

"That's Jack Laurent!"

Jack paused mid-step at the corner of Sixty-third and Madison on Tuesday afternoon and glanced down the busy, pedestrian-clogged sidewalk. She was already a little late to meet J.P. at Barneys and she didn't want to keep him waiting, especially since she'd spent her afternoon chemistry class formulating a plan.

And let's guess: The plan involves a certain *type* of chemistry?

A tubby-looking guy in a way-too-tight blue polo shirt and knee-skimming cargo shorts waddled up to her, waving wildly.

"Billboard girl!" The guy smiled in recognition, offering his hand for her to shake. Jack nodded dumbly, feeling like a deer trapped in headlights.

"What billboard, honey?" A tracksuit-sporting woman sidled up to the man. She quickly yanked a clunky Nikon from her shiny pink LeSportsac fanny pack and began taking photos of Jack. "Does anyone know who she is?" she yelled as a small crowd began curiously assembling around Jack.

"Hi," Jack began brilliantly. She felt very exposed and almost embarrassed. It wasn't like she was *famous* famous, so actually stopping to smile felt sort of cheesy and fake. "I'm sorry, I have to run."

No pictures please!

Jack hurriedly dashed across the street, eager to get away from her entourage and meet up with J.P. She had been ridiculously busy—Jeannette and Candice, the Cashman assistants, had set up an absurd schedule of shoots and appearances for her, culminating in the lofts' big launch party this Friday night, when the building would officially open its doors—and she and J.P. had only crossed paths at home. Today was pretty much the first time they'd actually be getting together outside of their apartment, and she was beyond happy to be free of Magellan. She was going to head to the fifth floor at Barneys, pick out some awesomely sexy lingerie while J.P. watched, and then tell him about her plan: that they'd do it—*it* it—on Friday night, after the party. It would be perfect.

"There you are, gorgeous!" J.P. broke through a Japanese tour group that was crowding the sidewalk, taking pictures of the iconic Barneys edifice. Jack smiled, her heart sinking slightly when he realized he was wearing his sweaty, ugly, polyester bright yellow Riverside Prep Squash T-shirt—again. The name of the sport was almost as ugly as the shirt itself.

"Hey!" Jack grabbed his arm and quickly pulled him toward the gold-plated door of Barneys. It wasn't like she was embarrassed by him, but the whole scene of meeting her high school boyfriend outside the store seemed a little cliché.

"Hold on! Let's let them take a picture!" J.P. gestured to the guy with the camera from across the street. "My dad'll be happy. He's really excited about all the press the lofts are getting," he explained.

Jack frowned. Hello? This was supposed to be the private moment where she was going to tell him she wanted to be ravaged?

Looks like someone didn't get the script.

"Let's go," Jack pouted, taking his wrist and dragging him through the doors. Instantly, she relaxed. So what if there were pervy guys on the street who recognized her. This was Barneys, her home away from home, a place where no one bothered you.

"Jack Laurent, darling!" A fortysomething woman approached, grabbing Jack's elbow. She wore a tight black Tocca suit and her hair was pulled back so tightly it looked like her eyes were popping out of her head. Her name tag read GLADYS. "So glad you came to us. Now that you're the new Manhattan It Girl, we'd love to show you some of our latest fall offerings," Gladys said, yanking Jack toward the Natura Bissé makeup counter.

"That's okay," Jack responded shortly. All she wanted to do was head upstairs and let J.P. pick out exactly which black La Perla underwear set he wanted to see her in. "Come on, J.P.," Jack added unnecessarily, her kitten heels clacking against the buffed marble floor as she led him to the banks of elevators.

"Jack Laurent, darling!" A tiny, spiky-haired sales associate appeared. He was only about five feet tall, so Jack completely towered over him. From above she could see his totally terrible bleached-blond dye job. "I'm such a huge fan of yours. I read on Page Six you were a dancer, but modeling is *much* more your speed. I've already picked out a bunch of dresses I could see you in—I know everyone will want to look like Jack this season!"

His name tag read MICK and he was practically jumping up and down like Magellan, who was probably peeing on her bed right now. "Can I *please* show you?" Mick begged. The cloying smell of Acqua di Parma seemed to emanate from his pores. "And of course, your boyfriend as well. You sure know how to pick them." Mick winked showily.

Jack stiffened. While free clothes sounded amazing in theory, something about his attitude made her feel naked and exposed.

And she was saving *that* for Friday night.

Jack shook her head, the mood broken. "You know, I think I'll have to come back another time. Thanks, Nick." Jack smiled tightly.

"Of course! And, um, it's Mick? Here's my card. Call me for *anything*," he added urgently. "I really want to be a stylist. I think we'd make a good team!"

Jack snorted to herself. "Let's go," she said shortly to J.P., who was standing awkwardly with his arms crossed in the ways guys do when they're tagging along on a shopping expedition with their girlfriends.

"I thought you needed something?" J.P. asked, sounding confused.

Jack shook her head definitively. "Nope. Come on!"

They burst back onto Madison, where a small crowd was still huddled near the entrance, obviously drawn to the guy with a camera like sharks to blood. Jack pulled down her Gucci aviators and tried to look busy and important. *Perfect*, she chanted to herself. It was her mantra, the word she used whenever she needed to nail a pirouette, ace a test, or just calm the fuck down.

"So, where to?" J.P. asked companionably, shifting gears from their aborted Barneys mission. He draped his arm over Jack's navy Sutton Studio cashmere sweater–covered shoulder. Jack wiggled away.

"Let's just go home," Jack said, crossing her arms over her

chest. Suddenly, she felt cold and exhausted and didn't know if she could face one more thing not going to plan.

"Sounds good." J.P. smiled broadly as he held his hand up to hail a taxi, not missing a beat. It was like it was all he'd wanted to do all along. Because maybe it was?

Jack tried to conceal a sigh. She wouldn't say no if J.P. suggested getting a drink at Rose Bar or dinner at Balthazar. But Jack knew he wouldn't. It wasn't until this week that she'd realized just how much J.P. loved hanging out at home. Maybe he'd always been like that, and she just hadn't noticed because they hadn't been living together.

As Jack got into the taxi and it sped downtown to the lofts, a wave of claustrophobia rushed over her. Genevieve, Sarah Jane, and Jiffy's nights were just beginning. They'd probably go for cocktails, followed by dinner, followed by more drinks at a bar and maybe a club. They could get home whenever they wanted, and they certainly didn't have to worry about coming home to dog pee in their sustainable bamboo beds.

But of course they could do what they wanted—they were single. And it wasn't like Jack wanted *that*. Besides, after Friday night, she and J.P. would definitely have something to do with all their free time at home.

That's the spirit.

a gets the buzz

"Name?" A burly bouncer stepped in front of Avery as she moved toward the glass door of Thom on Wednesday night, the bar where she was meeting James to talk about the Jack Laurent story. He didn't seem to think twice about taking the intern to drinks.

"Avery Carlyle," she said confidently, even though her heart was thumping against her chest. She was on the verge of a break-through, and she was determined not to let anything fuck it up. Maybe her first week at *Metropolitan* had sucked, and maybe she did have to work on a story about Jack, but she was working on it with a super-important journalist who took *her* seriously. She wore a scoop-back dress by The Row with gray suede pointed-toe ankle boots and had pulled her long wheat-blond hair into a messy bun at the nape of her neck in an effort to look serious and smart, yet sexy.

"Go on in. Your date is waiting for you," the bouncer said, his eyes flicking appreciatively up Avery's ensemble.

"Thanks." Avery walked through the door and down the nar-row, candlelit black spiral staircase into the bar. She couldn't believe she was actually here. Thom was an ultra-exclusive bar and eating club on Thompson Street in the West Village owned by Manhattan media mogul and billionaire Towson Wexler. Anyone who was anyone came here because not only did they have a firm no-cameras, no-BlackBerrys, no-blogging policy, but also the only way to get in was to call Towson's assistant and make a reservation.

"Aviary!"

Avery glanced over to see James waving to her from a low-slung black leather banquette in the corner. Avery smiled broadly, not even caring that his Scottish accent made her name sound like a home for birds.

Anything beats Intern.

James wore a paisley tie and a gray pin-striped Hickey Freeman suit, but instead of making him look totally gay, the paisley set off his sexy five o'clock stubble, giving him a slightly European look.

"Hi James," Avery said, sitting down next to him.

"A drink?" he asked, motioning to the waiter.

"Vodka gimlet," Avery confidently told the blond waitress, who nodded and slithered off. Vodka gimlets were what her grandmother always ordered, and to Avery were synonymous with sophistication and glamour.

"Vodka gimlet. You certainly are a Ticky trainee." James smirked, sipping from his water glass. Avery noticed he didn't have a drink. Weird. Instantly, the waitress came back and placed her drink on the black lacquer table in front of them.

"So tell me, Avery, which story of mine has been your favorite?" James asked, his blue eyes probing hers. He scooted closer to her on the bench so they were now seated on only one rigid black cushion. "I always love to hear what beautiful girls think of my writing."

Avery smiled like an idiot, racking her brain for an answer. In truth, she usually just skimmed the actual articles of *Metropolitan* and mostly focused on the fashion spreads. "You know, it's really hard to pick just one," Avery said, hoping that didn't sound too much like a cop-out. She glanced around the restaurant. Even on a Wednesday night, Barbara Walters sat in a booth, animatedly gesturing to a cowering white-haired man, while a group of long-haired models gossiped in a corner banquette.

James grinned. Avery smiled uncertainly back, batting her heavily mascaraed eyelashes and hoping he didn't think she was a total airhead.

"What's *your* favorite?" she asked, cringing before the sentence even left her mouth. It sounded like she was asking him what his favorite pet was. She grabbed her drink off the black lacquer table and downed half of it before she could ask him something even *more* embarrassing.

Like his age?

"Ah, the good old journalism 'answer a question with a question' method," James said.

"Yeah," Avery said nervously. This wasn't going as smoothly as she was hoping. Luckily, the bar was lit only by glass Tiffany lamps placed discreetly on side tables, so James couldn't see the blush that was beginning to spread from her chest up to her face. For a working meeting, this felt suspiciously like a date. Not like that was a bad thing. After all, her sister wasn't the only one who could score a European.

Ladies and gentlemen, welcome to the World Cup, Carlyle style.

"Well, I'll tell you, my favorite stories are the ones where we pull back the gilded curtain on Manhattan. I love uncovering people's motivations and desires," James said. "You New York girls start young!" His gaze flicked down to Avery's empty vodka gimlet. Yikes. She needed to remember to slow down. After all, this was *work*.

"So, tell me about you," James asked, leaning back against the stiff black leather cushions.

"Aren't you having anything to drink?" Avery couldn't resist asking.

"Don't drink on the job." James shrugged. "Long story. But you're an intern, so I say live it up. I promise, the alcohol when you're young can only help you. It just catches up once you turn thirty," James said ruefully. Avery wondered how old he was exactly. He looked younger than thirty to her.

"Well," Avery began, "I'm originally from Nantucket but my grandmother, Avery Carlyle the first, was a lifelong New Yorker. When she passed away, my family came here to settle her estate and so far, it's been a dream come true. Although it would have been so much better if my grandmother were still alive." Avery smiled sadly.

"Hmm," James said, fiddling with the straw in his water glass and sounding politely bored.

"I'm really enjoying New York," she added desperately. Great, now she sounded like a freaking tourist. Next thing she knew, she'd be asking him to take her on a tour of the Empire State Building.

"Yeah?" James asked lightly. "And let's get you another drink— you're all done," he said, motioning to a passing waitress. Avery liked that he was ordering for her.

"What have you been enjoying the most about the city?" James asked, leaning closer toward her.

"There are no rules," Avery blurted, backing away a few inches. Now that he seemed interested, she was a little confused. Did she like him? Was this a date? Too many questions were sloshing around her brain.

"No rules. Right-o!" James's eyes gleamed. "Like, how? Are those all-girl private schools the hotbeds of sin the media would have us believe?"

"Not really." Avery racked her brain, thinking of some type of story to tell James about her Constance Billard life. It wasn't like she'd exactly tell him her only friends were her sister and a pierced, tattooed girl who called herself flexual. "My friend Jiffy always crashes these VIP parties and dinners by RSVP'ing in her sister's name, and my other friend steals clothes from the fashion closet of the magazine her mom edits," Avery finally offered.

"Yeah, but that's schoolgirl stuff. I bet you do that too when you get the chance," James countered. "Tell me more about the wicked lives of you Upper East Siders."

"Well, we can get into *any* club in the city and no one checks IDs. My other friend Genevieve always dates these lame C-list Hollywood actors, but the only reason they go out with her is because her dad is a director." Avery crossed her legs.

"You need another drink!" James announced, motioning to the waitress, then dropping his hand on Avery's bare knee. Avery glanced down and saw he wasn't wearing a wedding ring. She felt her stomach leap.

Doesn't she mean *churn*?

"So, what else, darling?" James asked. Avery blinked, unable to focus. What had they been talking about before? It didn't matter. James had called her darling! Suddenly an elaborate fantasy of their life together spread out before her. They'd get married and be a literary power couple, capable of making or breaking people's reputations. They'd have lavish dinner parties at their classic-six apartment, where the Manhattan media elite would gather, the hottest ticket in town. "So, let's get down to business. How did the Cashman Lofts girl captivate New York?" James raised an eyebrow.

"You mean Jack?" Avery momentarily felt her mood darken. She'd like to talk about something else. Like herself. Or like herself and James. She hurriedly gulped down her vodka gimlet, realizing midway through it had just been refilled.

"She's . . . different," Avery said finally.

"How so? How did she wind up in that loft?"

"She has . . . special circumstances," Avery finished mysteriously. "She's close with her boyfriend's family. And, of course, she'd never be one to turn down a free apartment. Her own living situation was a little bit complicated. . . ." Avery trailed off.

"Well, her boyfriend must be head over heels for her to have his father give her an apartment, no?" James asked.

"Well, sort of . . ." Avery began, then paused. She certainly didn't know how close J.P. and Jack could be when just two weeks ago J.P. had been declaring his love for her sister.

"I don't really know if there's anything between them, so much as what J.P. has to offer. Or at least, what his *family* has to offer," Avery whispered confidentially. She clipped her words, trying not to slur. "Jack sort of finds opportunities. And I think having an apartment was important to her," she finished, thinking of the miserable attic Jack had been living in. Avery considered telling James about it, but stopped herself. Yeah, Jack had been a bitch to her, but there was no need to sink to her level.

"So, Dick Cashman must really like her then," James nodded.

"I guess so. I don't know why," Avery snorted, crossing her leg. All of a sudden, her foot made contact with her half-full glass, sending the liquid all over James's pants. "Christ! Fuck!" James swore, standing up. The spreading stain made it look like he'd peed his pants.

"Sorry!" Avery squeaked in horror. She frantically dabbed the area close to his crotch with a napkin, then stopped. Why was it that whenever something was going well with a guy, something went freakishly wrong? "I didn't mean to!"

"Don't worry!" James grabbed her hand, brought it to his mouth, and kissed it. "I think it was adorable. You're a little minx, I can tell."

Avery smiled numbly, not sure if she should smile or cry. At least James didn't think she was a *total* disaster.

"Fascinating stuff you were telling me." James shook his head. "But, I suppose I have to get you home, Cinderella," he said, helping Avery stand up.

What a fairy-tale ending.

From: gentlestrokin@gmail.com
To: SwimTeam_All@StJudes.edu
Date: Wednesday, October 20, 7:00pm
Subject: Swim Team Throwdown

Gentlemen,
The team's just not meshing, and that's affecting your performances in the pool. I'm hosting a pasta dinner at my apartment on Friday night at eight o'clock to get us all on the same page for the big meet against Unity on Saturday. Attendance is mandatory. Call Carlyle if you have questions.
—Coach

r parties like a dirty hippie

Rhys lay on his bed on Wednesday night, aimlessly tossing his Hacky Sack up and down. It was kind of cool the way the colors all merged together as it turned in the air, he thought. He pulled out the monogrammed Tiffany lighter he'd embarrassingly stolen from his dad's office and lit up the roach he had in his pocket. He couldn't tell if it was good or if it was—tapped out? Smoked out? He took a drag and held the smoke in until he could almost feel his lungs expand, then exhaled easily. It was as if his years of swimming had primed him for being a champion pot smoker. He'd been baked since the other day and finally, for the first time, felt relaxed. He'd skipped school to hang out in the park, and suddenly, he felt like the first sixteen years of his life had been a mistake.

"Rhys?" The strident voice of Lady Sterling carried down the hall.

"Come in," Rhys muttered, stuffing the Hacky Sack inside his Frette pillowcase. He certainly didn't want to wind up demonstrating his Hacky Sack skills on an episode of *Tea with Lady Sterling*.

What about his champion pot-smoking skills?

"Darling, we need to know if you're coming to the wedding this weekend? I know there are a lot of people who'd love to see you." Lady Sterling walked into his bedroom carrying a Domino's pizza box in one hand and Estella, one of her many corgis, in the other. At least it was probably Estella—they were kind of hard to tell apart. Usually the corgis spent all their time at the Sterling compound in Bedford unless Lady Sterling was shooting a segment with them.

"I'll take that," Rhys said, swinging his legs off the bed and grabbing the pizza box. He'd never had Dominos before, but after smoking up, it was all he could think about. It was like his life wouldn't be complete unless he had a pepperoni and pineapple pizza. And now it was here. Rhys grinned tenderly at the greasy cardboard container as he set it on his desk. Estella emitted a low-pitched whine of protest at being separated from the pizza.

"You ordered that? I thought it had been a mistake, but . . ." Lady Sterling shook her head sadly, her gold Cartier necklaces clinking against each other.

"Thanks, Mom!" Rhys added, hoping Lady Sterling would just go away. Luckily, the pungent smell of pepperoni and greasy cheese seemed to mask the thick scent of pot that Rhys was sure was clinging to him.

"You could have had Anka make something." Lady Sterling narrowed her eyes. Anka was their stern Romanian housekeeper and the only person in the world who could stand up to Lady Sterling.

"Ah well, you're a growing boy, so I suppose it's fine. Right, Estella?" Lady Sterling cooed toward the dog, who was clawing her way out of Lady Sterling's arms, desperate to get to the pizza.

"Thanks again, Mom!" Rhys repeated himself desperately, hoping that she'd take the hint and leave.

Instead, Lady Sterling sniffed the air suspiciously. "Are you planting something in here? It almost smells like the herb garden," she mused.

Wonder why?

"Um, no," Rhys said uncomfortably. God, he was hungry. The smell of the cheese wafting from the pizza box was practically killing him.

"Okay, then. Well, I'm off to prepare for the trip back across the pond! And I do wish you'd reconsider coming with us. I was speaking with your father and we thought maybe if you came, we could tour a few of the schools over there. Boarding school might be what you need, although of course, I'd miss you terribly. . . ." Lady Sterling trailed off.

"I'm fine," Rhys said, shaking his head. It was true. Ever since he'd met the Darrow kids, everything had seemed so much *easier.*

That happens when you skip out on everything hard.

"Ah, well, your father and I may do a tour ourselves, then. You know he loves to relive his boarding school days." Lady Sterling shook her head fondly. "Feel free to invite some of the swim team fellows over while we're gone. Even if you're not on the team anymore, you've known those boys for years. You seem like you need some cheering up. You can have Anka prepare," Lady Sterling offered. She looked softly at her son. "I know things have been hard for you lately."

Oh, she has no idea.

"Thanks, Mom." Rhys nodded, not looking up until he heard the sound of his mother's Prada flats disappearing down the cherrywood hallway. He hurriedly stood up, shut the door, and locked it for good measure.

He pulled up the white top of the flimsy pizza box and inhaled the scent of the cheese. He placed a slice in his mouth with one hand, logging on to his e-mail with the other.

Swim Team Throwdown, read the subject line of the only e-mail in his inbox. He clicked on it. Grease fell on the keyboard as he scanned the e-mail announcing a pasta party for the team before their big meet against Unity. Suddenly the greasy cheese in Rhys's mouth made him feel sick.

Fuck it. Fuck the swim team and their lame parties. Rhys scrolled down to the bottom of the e-mail and deftly hit the unsubscribe link to make sure he wouldn't get any more e-mails about the swim team. He didn't need them. In fact, he was going to throw his *own* party. With his *real* friends. He opened another e-mail, typing in Lucas's address to spread the word. Maybe he and Lisa would end up being lovers and have hippie babies and then move to Canada and live on a farm and raise alpacas. Snowboarding alpacas.

Aw, don't we love stoner daydreams?

house and garden

"Hurry!" Jack hissed at the cabbie through clenched teeth. It was Wednesday evening, and instead of a night of drinking and gossiping with Sarah Jane and Genevieve at an exclusive MoMA garden party, she was freaking out in the back of a cab, racing back down to her apartment in Tribeca. She'd been planning to talk to the girls about J.P.'s annoying new domesticity while smoking cigarettes and getting way too drunk on rosé in the sculpture garden. She felt like she'd aged thirty years in a weekend, and had been looking forward to just acting like a dumb teenager for the night. But instead, she'd received a phone call from J.P. as soon as the skinny, bitchy girl manning the door had allowed her in. He'd called to tell her that he and his parents were expecting her for dinner at *her* apartment. She'd had to leave Sarah Jane and Genevieve, who had been flirting with a cute older guy with a Scottish accent, and hail a cab in the middle of the absurd midtown evening traffic. Now they were finally almost downtown.

"Here's fine!" Jack practically screamed as the cabbie almost sailed past the building. She stuffed a twenty in his fist and ran inside, her Chanel flats clacking against the wood floors of the lobby. It was decorated in different shades of wood, making it look like a ski château in the Alps or some luxe hideaway near the Grand Canyon. A waterfall made of rainwater was the focal point, and different types of Japanese cherry trees dotted the perimeter. Not like Jack was pausing to appreciate her surroundings. All she cared about was making it to her apartment to make sure anything hideously embarrassing, like her underwear or tampons or the half-eaten tube of raw cookie dough in the fridge, was hidden before J.P.'s parents got there.

"Miss, I just sent your guests up!" the night doorman announced grandly.

"Fuck!" Jack whispered under her breath, breaking into a run toward the elevator. *Perfect, perfect, perfect,* she chanted to the same rhythm as her heartbeat as the elevator door slid closed.

The door to the elevator opened into her apartment and Jack could hear the loud, Russian-accented voice of J.P.'s mom.

"Hi!" Jack exclaimed, hoping she didn't sound out of breath or seem too sweaty. The back of her Marc Jacobs organic cotton jersey dress, received in yesterday's mail as a housewarming present from a nearby boutique, felt moist against her back. Yuck.

"Eez beautiful!" Tatyana Cashman tottered over to Jack and planted a kiss on her cheek. Jack smiled, not sure if Tatyana was referring to her or the loft.

Or the billboard picture of her *in* the loft?

"You like your palace, Jackie, baby?" Dick Cashman asked jovially, settling into one of the elegant white organic cotton–covered wingback chairs in the center of the apartment. The chair groaned slightly under his weight.

"It's amazing," Jack mumbled. Candice and Jeannette, the

robot-twin publicity assistants, were sitting on one of the teak and hemp couches in the corner, looking over dozens of print-outs.

"Hey, gorgeous!" J.P. said, walking out of her bathroom and wiping his hands on the sides of his Diesel jeans.

Jack smiled tightly at J.P., trying to send him a psychic message that she—that *this*—was not okay. Now that they'd all made themselves comfortable, maybe they could explain what the fuck they were doing in her apartment?

"Good!" Dick boomed. "So, we're trying to figure out the snacks for our little shindig on Friday and I thought, might as well see how you're settling in. Considering you're part of the family and all." He nodded. Just then, Jack realized that a swarm of caterers were huddled by the kitchen on the other end of the apartment.

"Well, I'm surprised." Jack smiled at Dick before glaring at J.P. He shrugged his shoulders slightly in a *don't blame me, this was his idea* way. She noticed her peach-colored La Perla camisole lying in a rumpled pile next to the white, organic cotton overstuffed English sofa. Jack hastily edged it under the couch with the tip of her boot.

"Glad you're making yourself at home!" Dick Cashman exclaimed as he triumphantly held up a wrinkled Snickers wrapper that he'd found wedged in the cushion. "I like ladies who eat!" he boomed, winking one bulging eye at Tatyana, who was absentmindedly stroking her blond, volumized hair as if it were a pet. Jack looked down and saw two of J.P.'s gross, slobbery puggles running around the apartment, trailed by Magellan. They'd better be housebroken.

"I'll take that." Jack snatched the wrapper from him.

"So, we're having dinner?" she asked desperately. She felt like she was supposed to play hostess, even though she had no idea who the caterers were, what they were making, or what Dick's PR bitches were doing here.

"Well, I think this experiment was a success. You're the talk of the town!" Dick crowed, glancing around the apartment in approval. "What do you say we sample these snacks? My problem is, they always cut the food so small at these fancy parties they don't give anyone a chance to really dig in!" Dick boomed as he led the group to the glass-topped dining room table. Instantaneously, the caterers converged around them, plunking down various plates of delicate-looking miniature quiches, beef skewers, sushi rolls, mini lamb burgers, and elegantly crafted bite-size prosciutto sandwiches. Jack's stomach rumbled, and she wished she could dig in without all these people around.

"Are you treating my beautiful boy all right? He is so much happier and healthier with you than with that messy little hippie girl," Tatyana said, squeezing Jack's knee and sticking three mini-quiches in her mouth. Jack smiled, despite herself. Maybe having J.P.'s parents here wasn't *too* bad.

Just then, her cell erupted into the first strains of *The Nutcracker*.

"That's my ballerina!" Dick announced randomly, grabbing several more lamb burgers.

"Sorry!" Jack mouthed, turning away from the table as she fished her phone from her black Marc Jacobs satchel. She frowned at the unfamiliar number on the display, wondering if it was a request for an interview or something.

"Hello?" she asked.

"Jacqueline Laurent?" An elderly sounding wavery voice asked, pronouncing her name as if it were two first names.

"Yes," she replied brusquely.

"This is the School of American Ballet. We wanted to let you know that the board was extremely impressed with your audition a few weeks ago. We're thrilled to offer you a scholarship in our apprentice company. Do you have any questions?"

"No. Thank you!" Jack breathed, shutting her phone as if she were in a dream. In the middle of everything, she'd almost forgotten about ballet and the scholarship audition she'd had to do after her father cut her off. She was *back*! She couldn't wait for her feet to hit the sleek black stage of Lincoln Center, to hear applause after a particularly difficult jump combination, to know that people were applauding her not only for her looks and poise, but for her talent. Her *real* talent. She grinned widely to herself, grabbing the glass of Veuve that had appeared in front of her as if by magic.

"Celebration?" Dick asked hopefully, his own glass of Veuve cocked in the air.

"I got a scholarship for ballet," she burbled happily, grinning at J.P., knowing he'd understand. He'd always known how important ballet was to her, that it separated her from other girls and made her special, made her unique, made her *Jack*.

"Scholarship? Well, hell!" Dick suddenly looked enraged, his beefy red neck straining against his pink hand-tailored shirt. He looked like a wealthy rancher who'd just found out all his cows had run off the range. "We can't have J.P.'s girl on scholarship! I'll buy the ballet! What's it called? The American Ballet Company? How much?" Dick reached into his pocket and pulled out a gold Montblanc pen and a leather-bound checkbook.

"Um, dad?" J.P. gave Jack's hand a reassuring squeeze. "This is Jack's thing. She earned it." Jack smiled, grateful that he understood.

"You can't buy the ballet, Dick," Jack said hurriedly. "It doesn't really work that way. It's sort of an honor to get a scholarship from them," she added, looking around the skeptical faces of Tatyana, Jeannette, and Candice.

"Nonsense. I'll buy you the whole city! It's your oyster and I'm happy to pay for it, Jackie baby! You're the love of J.P.'s life. What's ours is yours," Dick said grandly. As if to underscore the point, one of the chefs marched in and plunked down a large tray of pigs in a blanket.

Jeannette and Candice simultaneously wrinkled their noses. "We said *festive*. This isn't festive—the entire menu looks like we're catering for the circus," Jeanette exclaimed, following the caterer into the kitchen.

"Are you okay, sweetie?" Tatyana asked suspiciously, placing her hand on Jack's arm. Jack nodded uneasily. She wished she could just escape, but she had nowhere else to go—this was her home now. J.P. smiled at her reassuringly, and she relaxed. Everything was *fine*.

"Jackie's just a little overwhelmed," Dick narrated, his red face gleaming in the candlelight. "And I don't know about you ladies, but I like these little franks!" To prove his point, he shoved two in his mouth.

Jack smiled. So what if J.P.'s parents saw her apartment as an extension of their own? At least she and J.P. understood each other. Everything was *perfect*.

Until she finds the surprise one of the puggles left in her Sigerson Morisson pumps.

gossipgirl.net

Disclaimer: All the real names of places, people, and events have been altered or abbreviated to protect the innocent. Namely, me.

hey people!

One of the hazards of my job is that everyone assumes that just because I dish the dirt, I can help them sift through their *own* dirt. But, my pets, as much as you may wish it, let me remind you that even though it seems like I have all the answers, I'm neither a therapist nor a psychic. I can't tell you that you're dating a stoner because you have latent daddy issues, that you wear all black as a retaliation against your control freak mom, or that the reason you insist on keeping your bangs so long is your warped desire to not see the world for what it really is.

Here's what I can tell you: All the absurd, self-defeating, and ultimately embarrassing things we end up doing are a result of human nature. We're all hardwired to dip a toe in the dark side of our psyches. Just make sure you don't venture too far away from shore, because then it becomes hard to swim back.

sightings

O and his coach, heading into a closed-door meeting in the St. Jude's athletic director's office. Swim meet strategy planning? . . . **R** on St. Mark's in the East Village, buying a Legalize Pot T-shirt. He has so much to learn about stoner style! . . . **J** and **J.P.**'s dad, having glasses of Côtes du Rhône in the lobby of the **Cashman Lofts**. To discuss the Cashman Lofts launch party . . . or to discuss something else? They do say French girls like older men. . . . **A** furiously scribbling whatever **S.J.** and

G were whispering about in French class. Watch out, ladies. We've got a reporter in our midst.

your e-mail

q: GG,
Working on a hot story and need your input. Call me, dollface.
—metrowriter

a: Dear Metro Writer,
Sorry, I don't do in-person interviews and certainly not on such short notice!
—GG

q: Dear Gossip Girl,
How much is the maximum age difference between a guy and a girl for it not to be super sketchy? Our health teacher, who's like 25 and has an 18-year-old boyfriend, tells us the formula is the older person's age, divided by two, plus seven is the minimum age the younger person can be. So, like, 25 divided by two is 12.5, and plus 7 is almost 20, which makes it totally okay. Is this right?
—math gurl

a: Dear MG,
Well, math isn't my strong suit, but let's put it this way. If one person has a curfew and the other doesn't, then it's probably not going to work.
—GG

Okay, as they say in therapy lingo: Time's up! Until next time, feel free to indulge in any of my favorite stress-reducers: champagne, a hot bath, or an afternoon nap. Note that all of the above should be done with a member of the opposite sex for maximum effectiveness.

You know you love me.

gossip girl

no press is bad press

Avery pushed open the glass doors to the *Metropolitan* offices on Thursday afternoon, eager to see James in the light of day. She'd spent the whole morning obsessing over their evening at Thom. Was he flirting with her? Had she gotten too tipsy?

Generally, when you have to ask yourself that question, the answer is yes.

She plopped her purple Lanvin hobo bag on top of her intern desk, not even caring about the bags of crap McKenna and Gemma had left for her to messenger to Barneys or wherever. She had better things to do than play slave to the assistants. Instead, she immediately picked up the large layout sheets of a new *Metropolitan* article.

All in the Family? read the headline, printed in Old English gothic font, as if it were some sort of formal announcement. In smaller letters, a sentence underneath read, *Is Jack Laurent sleeping her way to the top of Cashman Lofts?* A photo alongside the text was of Jack and J.P. kissing in front of Barneys. Jack seemed to be looking warily at the camera, while J.P.'s eyes were closed, his expression totally blissful.

She turned to the next page. There, in bold letters next to a photo of Jack's billboard, was a quote Avery recognized as her own, vodka-infused words. SOME PEOPLE HAVE SPECIAL CIRCUMSTANCES THEY'D LIKE TO HIDE. Next to that was a photo of the Cashman Lofts with an inset picture of a ruddy, lobster-colored Dick Cashman merrily toasting Jack Laurent. Jack was smiling and looked beautiful. MAY-DECEMBER ROMANCE? read the caption underneath the photo.

"Looking good, right?"

Avery whirled around to see James smiling down at her. "Not just the article," James murmured, his gaze flicking appreciatively to Avery's low-cut silk Tocca blouse.

"I didn't realize this would come out so soon," Avery squeaked. She felt a tiny pang of regret as she stared at the photo of Dick and Jack. It implied that they were having some sort of illicit affair, and that her relationship with J.P. was just a cover-up. But the article never *explicitly* said that. And besides, none of the quotes—about Jack's special circumstances and secretive behavior—were false.

Is she sure she doesn't want to go into politics?

"It's a great story." James smiled proudly. "Read it through and let me know if there's anything that needs adding. We make a good team. I already told Ticky, and she agrees." James squeezed her shoulder and Avery's knees felt weak.

"And look what I did for you." James flicked the layout with his thumb and forefinger, making a thwacking sound. *Additional reporting by Avery Carlyle*. Avery grinned. In print, her name looked pretty cool. She bit her Lancôme-glossed lip to try to suppress a smile. She wanted James to see her as blasé, like she got bylines in major cultural magazines all the time.

"You know how many interns get bylines here?" James asked rhetorically, making a zero with his thumb and forefinger. "I'm looking out for you. And I'll pick you up and bring you to the Cashman Lofts party tomorrow. See if there's anything we want to slam into the story."

"Cool!" Avery said, cringing at how teenager-y she sounded. "I mean, I can't wait," she added. This time, she'd just limit herself to one—maybe two—glasses of champagne.

"Great." James smiled, displaying his mega-white teeth. "Now, can you be an angel and head down to the cafeteria? I'd love a large tea with lemon. I'd hate for all your recent success to go to your pretty head." He ruffled Avery's hair and carelessly tossed a rumpled bill on her overflowing desk. "There's a fiver. Keep the change."

Avery stuffed the crumpled bill in her purse. Even the way he ordered her around was cute.

If you're into that sort of thing.

Her heart raced, imagining what would happen when the article hit newsstands. Jack already hated her. So what if the article made it look like she was trading sex for real estate? Maybe that's what Jack got for being a self-centered, histrionic bitch. As she strutted to the elevator, Avery allowed a victory smile to seep onto her face.

Game on?

physical therapy

"Carlyle, hold up a sec," Coach Siegel yelled, crouching down next to Owen's lane and tapping his hand against the wall so he'd stop swimming. Owen yanked his goggles off his face and glanced up at Coach's mouthwash-blue eyes.

"Hey there. I don't know what's going on, but you've got to get yourself together. You've got to get the *team* together."

Owen nodded. As if he needed another reminder that the team hated him.

"Here, get out. Let's take a walk," Coach said. He blew the whistle so the rest of the guys stopped swimming. "Guys, do a five hundred timed free. Honor system." He blew the whistle again and one by one the guys sprinted off the walls and down the lane lines. Owen pulled himself out of the pool and followed Coach over to a secluded corner by the lifeguard stands.

"What's going on?" Coach asked. "I don't really know why Sterling quit, but his leaving affected everyone. We need to pull the team together."

"It's not that easy," Owen mumbled. Over in the water, what

had begun as a serious swim set had devolved into some weird water polo game, using Chadwick's goggles as a ball.

"Look, I know there's some drama between you and Sterling over his lady. Right?" Coach looked Owen in the eye. "You stole his girl?"

"Not exactly," Owen muttered, gazing at the intersecting black and white tiles of the pool deck to avoid looking at Coach. He didn't remember ever having a conversation like this with his high school coach back in Nantucket. Owen felt a pang of homesickness for his tiny, sandy hometown.

"Okay, well, I don't really care what happened between you two in your personal life. I *do* care that whatever happened is affecting my team. You're not firing on all cylinders, Carlyle," Coach said sternly, not even noticing when a bikini-clad lifeguard passed two feet away from them and climbed up on the lifeguard stand. Coach *always* noticed the guards who wore bikinis.

"I want you to take the afternoon off to think about this and come up with some ideas for how you'll pull the team together. I'm serious, Carlyle." Coach stood up, clearly indicating their meeting was over. Owen wordlessly walked into the locker room and changed in one of the lone bathroom stalls in the corner. Normally, the only people who changed in the stalls were the JV guys who were terrified of the random hazing carried out by Hugh, usually involving permanent markers. Owen just didn't want to run into any of his teammates.

He slid his iPhone from his maroon St. Jude's swim team bag. Three missed calls. All from Kelsey. Just thinking of her coral lips made him feel okay. He heard Coach's voice ringing in his ears. He knew that being with Kelsey was hurting his relationship with his teammates. But . . . fuck it. It was like *Romeo and Juliet.* They would be together, even if no one else wanted them to be.

Galvanized, he hailed a cab outside the Ninety-second Street Y. Kelsey only lived on Seventy-seventh, but he wanted to see her *now.*

Coming over, miss you, he texted, and leaned back in the cab. He wished he could whisk Kelsey away to an uninhabited island. He'd swim every morning and then they'd go foraging for food and fall asleep, intertwined on the beach.

Okay, Mr. *Lost.*

Finally, the cab swept up to Kelsey's green-awninged building. A doorman stood at rapt attention and the doorway was flanked by two stone lion sculptures that seemed to be glaring at Owen. He walked inside the building and paused at the reception desk.

"Um, I'm here to see Kat—Kelsey Talmadge," he corrected himself.

"I'll call her," the doorman said, picking up an old phone and dialing. "Go on up, she's expecting you."

Owen rode the elevator and made his way to the end of the hallway. Suddenly the door to her apartment opened and Kelsey burst out, wearing her plaid Seaton Arms skirt and a black cashmere sweater.

"You're here!" she exclaimed, as if she hadn't seen Owen in weeks, rather than hours. Owen let his fingers play against her smooth shoulders, but then he pulled away.

"Are you okay?" Kelsey bit her pink lip suggestively. She pulled her strawberry blond hair up, into a ponytail, then dropped it around her face and smiled. "I know how to make you feel better," she added coyly, wrapping her fingers around Owen's wrist and pulling him inside her apartment, which was decorated in slate grays and blacks. It was so neutral it was hard to imagine anyone really living here. There were no bookshelves or artwork or sculpture collections. He paced back and forth awkwardly, finally perching on the edge of an overstuffed gray sofa. Kelsey followed him and sat down in his lap.

"No, wait!" Owen pushed her delicate hip off his lap so they were seated side by side. He needed to know if this was for real. And to do that, they couldn't just hook up right away.

"What?" Kelsey's blue eyes widened in confusion. Her eyes reminded Owen of the ocean—wide and deep, and difficult to know what was going on below the surface.

Is anything going on below the surface?

"Yeah, I just had a crappy swim practice," Owen said. He looked around. He didn't even know who Kelsey lived with. Did she have any brothers or sisters? Pets?

Aren't they a little beyond these questions?

"How long have you lived here?" Owen asked lamely. It was too quiet in here.

"Two years. Before that I lived in Brooklyn. This is my step-dad's place." Kelsey smiled a half smile, as if Owen was trying to play a game and she didn't know the rules yet.

"Are we done with twenty questions?" she asked teasingly. Owen jammed his hands in his tracksuit pocket, feeling incredibly frustrated. He was so confused right now. He wanted Kelsey. But he also wanted to get to *know* Kelsey.

Aren't boys supposed to be simple?

"Let's go to my room. I can try to make you feel better." Kelsey grabbed the crook of Owen's elbow and yanked him down a long hallway that was covered with artsy black-and-white prints of the city. "No one's home, it's fine," she explained, as if that was why

Owen was hesitating. She opened the fourth door on the hallway and pulled him inside.

"Kiss me!" she demanded, resting her hands against the back of the door as if she wanted Owen to trap her.

"This is nice." Owen desperately tried to ignore Kelsey's devour-me attitude. He pretended to study a charcoal drawing hanging on the wall. It was of a group of kids sitting on the steps of a brownstone, and was actually pretty good. One of the girls sort of looked like Kelsey, complete with her crooked incisor and wispy hair around her ears. "That looks like you," he continued.

"That's because it *is* me," Kelsey explained. She shrugged off her sweater to expose her creamy white shoulders, and lay down on the bed. "You can get a better view of it over here," Kelsey called to Owen, pulling on his arm.

"Wait, no!" Owen yanked his wrist away from her thin fingers. He saw an expression of hurt cross her face and instantly felt bad. "I just want to get to know you!" He sat down next to her and held her hand with his.

"I think we know each other pretty well." Kelsey took the hand that Owen was playing with and stroked his cheek.

"Let's play a game, okay. No touching until we've learned five things about each other," he invented, pulling Kelsey's hand away. "First, what's the story with that drawing?"

Kelsey glanced at her gray walls. "I drew it a couple years ago. It's all right." She shrugged. Owen glanced up at it again. She did? He didn't know she was an artist. Owen looked more closely at the pictures of what seemed to be a Brooklyn streetscape, complete with brownstones and tree-lined streets. "Is that where you lived?"

"Why do you care?" Kelsey giggled. "Okay, if we're playing your game, I guess it's your turn. Go." She rolled her eyes.

"Thanks." Owen dredged his memory for something. "When I was little, you know how most kids have stuffed animals? I had a pet rock. It was a wish rock—one of those ones that has a band of sand around it that's a different color. This one was brown and white, and you're supposed to throw them in the ocean and make a wish, but I used to sleep with it. Except I lost it when I was ten. I know it sounds crazy, but I still miss it. I sometimes used to walk on the beach, looking for one like it," Owen blathered, stopping abruptly. An awkward silence filled the room.

"That's . . . cute," Kelsey said finally, looking at him strangely. "But I know what's better than a pet rock . . ." she suggested, nuzzling her pert, freckly nose against Owen's chiseled chin. Owen halfheartedly kissed her back. This wasn't working.

"You know, I'm not feeling too well," Owen said lamely. "I'll call you," he promised, springing up from her bed and practically running to the elevator. He ignored the raised eyebrows of the doorman and burst out the door, only feeling free as he jogged next to the elm tree–lined path by Central Park. He dodged strollers and dog walkers and only stopped running once he saw his building. He breathed a deep sigh of relief. It was good to be home.

b makes a sartorial statement

Baby nervously adjusted Avery's Hermès scarf that she used as a headband and surveyed the other Thursday afternoon patrons of the Hungarian Pastry Shop. She'd spent the last two days reading Sydney's mom's book. She'd thought it would be lame and self-help-y, but it actually made sense. Basically, all Lynn advocated was militant and consistent cleaning and purging stuff, to make sure your past selves and goals wouldn't invade your future plans. As soon as she'd finished, she'd begged Sydney to set up a meeting, just so she could pick Lynn's brain about what she could possibly do to fulfill her therapy requirement. She'd canceled her chakra-balancing life coach hippie appointment, so, really, Lynn was her last hope. The coffee shop was a popular Columbia hangout, filled with students and professors, all enjoying caffeine and late-afternoon sunshine. She shivered in the outdoor seating area and shifted her uneven wooden chair back and forth on the cement.

"Baby?"

"Lynn?" Baby guessed shyly. She looked exactly as she did in her author photo, with shiny brown hair pulled back into a no-nonsense ponytail and tortoiseshell Prada glasses perched on her head. Baby pushed the worn wooden table away so there'd be room for Lynn to squeeze into a seat.

"I'm telling you, Baby, I need a good cup of oolong. Ever have that feeling?" Lynn asked, settling on the rickety wooden chair. Baby nodded happily. Her mom always used to make oolong for the triplets on snow days.

"Good." Lynn nodded. "Some oolong!" she bellowed, even though it didn't seem like a server was anywhere nearby. "And some cookies or something. Carbs!" she commanded. "So, what can I do for you?" She widened her large, brown eyes. They were the same caramel color as Sydney's.

"It's just . . ." Baby began, feeling surprisingly shy. She gazed across the street. Leaves were starting to turn on the small, spindly trees on the sidewalk, and people were hurrying by with their heads down. Baby shivered slightly, pulling her sweatshirt closer to her. "I think I'm unfocused," Baby said finally. That sounded much better than saying she was addicted to men.

"How so?"

The server put down a pot of tea, two mugs, and a plate of assorted cookies. The mugs were mismatched and chipped, and Baby's said *World's Greatest Grandma* on the side. Lynn expertly took the pot and splashed tea into the mugs.

"Well, I was seeing this guy back in Nantucket, and I thought we were in love, but then I moved *here* and started hanging out with this really nice, really sweet guy who was just way too different from me, so we broke up, and then I ended up following another guy to Barcelona and he wasn't even there. That's why I have to be in therapy. I kind of skipped a week of school," Baby admitted ruefully. She hoped her romantic history didn't sound too slutty for Lynn. It was like a *Clockwork Orange* cycle of dating and ditching guys.

"Mrs. McLean gave you mandatory therapy. Interesting," Lynn mused, leaning back and appraising Baby.

"Yeah, but I haven't found anyone who can help me. I mean, I'm not against therapy—it's just that I don't think anyone can figure out what's wrong with me. Do you think maybe you could?" Baby asked, nervously chewing the frayed sleeve of her sweatshirt.

"How long have you had that sweatshirt?" Lynn asked randomly, ignoring Baby's question.

"It used to be my ex's. It's warm," Baby said coldly. What did that have to do with *anything*? She took another sip of oolong.

"Get rid of it." Lynn nodded definitively. Baby narrowed her eyes. *What?* She reached down to pull a few dollars out of her bag for the tea. She didn't want to sit here and listen to this. Of course this was just another waste of time.

"Sydney said you read my book," Lynn said, looking amused at Baby's rising anger. "It's all in chapter three. I don't think there's anything wrong with you, but I do think you have some things holding you back. What you need to do is embrace your life now. Love who you are! What does that sweatshirt symbolize?"

Baby glanced down at the ragged sleeve edge. Her ex-boyfriend, Tom, also used to chew on it, usually before he told a lie. Looking back, the habit was gross, not endearing at all.

"I guess it symbolizes Nantucket. Having a boyfriend. Being accepted for who I was." Baby shrugged. She'd never really thought about it. She'd never been one for material possessions. "Is this really why I'm not finding myself?" Baby asked suddenly.

"Well, honey, that shirt's not doing you any favors!" Lynn bellowed. Several people at the next table looked over to stare. "Tell you what, sweetie. Go home and clean out your closet. Get rid of anything that doesn't make you feel like *you*." Lynn nodded thoughtfully.

Let-go-of-retail therapy?

"Do you think it'll really work?" Baby asked in a small voice. Suddenly, she wished she could take her question back. She didn't want Lynn to think she was being rude—it was just that her solution seemed so . . . obvious. Simple.

"I'm the expert, Baby. But don't be so serious—just have fun! And here's the other thing," Lynn went on. "Once you begin tossing stuff, you need to begin *organizing*. Pastel with pastel. Black with black. Jeans with jeans. Short sleeves, long sleeves." Lynn looked up sharply, as if to make sure Baby was paying attention. Baby nodded vigorously.

"A little categorization never hurt anyone," she added as she bit into a cookie. Baby noticed she chewed with her mouth open, just like Sydney.

"I don't own any pastels," Baby admitted.

"More power to you!" Lynn cocked her mug at Baby as if she were toasting her. "Now, down to what you were talking about before. That Spanish guy?" Lynn asked, shoving an entire chocolate chip cookie in her mouth.

"Mateo," Baby said. It was funny. She barely remembered what he looked like now. Did he have brown hair? Black? She couldn't quite get a mental image of him. Instead, on the screen in her mind, she just saw herself: crazily riding a Vespa through the Gaudí park in Barcelona with a bunch of off-duty waiters she'd met on the beach. Streaking through fountains with Sydney on one of their Underground Response events. Running along a dark and turbulent ocean, looking out into the endless horizon and imagining a whole world of adventure. "I think I liked the idea of him more," Baby added, suddenly feeling weird about discussing her love life with her friend's *mom*.

"Well, see what you think of him after you do some clutter control." Lynn nodded sagely. "Now, I'm sure you have better things to do than hang out with me all afternoon." Lynn rummaged through her bag and pulled out a copy of the *New Yorker*. Obviously, the meeting was over.

"Thank you!" Baby said. Lynn nodded, grabbing Baby's practically untouched teacup.

"No problem!" Lynn waved her away, drinking the rest of Baby's tea. Baby turned the corner onto 110th Street. She was cold, but she yanked off her sweatshirt anyway and threw it in a trash can.

Hallelujah!

come one, come all, to a stoned-soul picnic

Rhys awkwardly puffed from the joint he'd tried to roll in his room. He wasn't sure if it was working, and the paper kept sticking to his chapped lips. He sighed in frustration. At least his parents had left for the wedding in England this morning. He'd skipped school and was just waiting for his new friends to come over.

The doorbell rang. Finally. Rhys inspected himself in the mirror. He hadn't bothered to take a shower today, so his dark brown hair was spiky and unkempt, he was still wearing a pair of old Patagonia athletic shorts and a gray Nike shirt he usually only ran in, and his eyes were all bloodshot.

At least this time it's not from crying.

He paused. The old Rhys would have taken a shower and pulled on a Ralph Lauren sweater. But this was the new Rhys. His friends accepted him for who he was. He bounded down the stairs and opened the heavy oak door in the foyer. Standing there were Lucas, Malia, and Vince, trailed by a crew of other unshowered, unshaven kids Rhys had never met.

"Come on in," Rhys said enthusiastically, flinging the door open.

"Thanks, man!" Lucas said eagerly, pumping Rhys's hand up and down. He was wearing a kid-size green T-shirt that said DON'T MESS WITH TEXAS and grass-stained khakis, and smelled like a mix of patchouli, pot, and Gorgonzola cheese. Lucas reverentially took off his shoes and placed them next to an antique grandfather clock.

"Word," he said, as if addressing the clock. "So, this is the casa? Nice, man!"

The kids behind him murmured appreciatively as they wandered in.

"Are more people coming?" Rhys asked nervously. He'd expected four or five kids, but now there were at least ten scattering throughout the town house. Lucas nodded distractedly, entranced by the small marble Italian greyhound sculpture housed in an eave under the stairs. "Hey, little buddy!" Lucas said, enthusiastically rubbing the sculpture's head.

Okay. Rhys needed pot, stat. "Hey, um, guys?" he called hesitantly, hoping they'd all come back. "I thought we could hang out up on the roof," he began awkwardly. He figured they could smoke up there. Besides, they couldn't make *too* much of a mess if they were all in one spot.

"Look at this!" Vince exclaimed, running back to the foyer holding a gold-topped cane that he'd obviously found in Lord Sterling's study. He was shoeless and was enjoying skidding on the buff-polished floors on his socks.

"Put that back!" Rhys called frantically, pulling it out of Vince's hand. "I mean, actually, I'll take it. Guys, let's just go upstairs to the greenhouse." A note of panic rose in his voice.

"Follow me," he commanded, leading the motley group over to the stairs. The greenhouse was a small construction Lady

Sterling insisted on installing on the roof. Not only did she use it for her own personal gardening, she occasionally used it as a location for her show. Right now, she was growing heirloom tomatoes for "Terrific Tomatoes," an annual fall segment.

"Here we are," Rhys finally said as they reached the enclosed terrace. It was private, which was key, and also had heat lamps, so there was no need for any of them to go downstairs even when it got colder out.

"Nice!" Lucas cried, immediately flinging open the greenhouse door.

"Don't!" Rhys called. He could see his mother's rows and rows of tomatoes, stretching up toward the hydroponic lights she'd had installed.

"Oh my God, they're tomatoes!" Malia called, enthralled.

"Yeah, but it's kind of hot in there. Come over here!" Rhys called, trying to entice them to the other side of the terrace, which had comfy lounge chairs and big planters full of mums.

"No, man, here's where the magic is," Lucas countered, pulling out a joint. "You want?"

Rhys hesitantly walked over. As long as he was watching them, how much harm could they do? All they needed to do was smoke up so they could chill out. He took the joint from Lucas's outstretched hand and took a long drag. There, that was so much better. "You want?" he asked Lisa, holding the joint out to her. Lisa wore a threadbare skirt that showed her unshaven legs. She giggled as she took it.

"Look at this." Lucas plucked one of the tomatoes and reverentially rolled it around his hand. "It's so beautiful and, like, so fragile. Like, squeeze it." He held it out to Rhys.

"Yeah, squeeze it," Malia whispered, staring intently at the tomato in Rhys's hand. They were all looking at him. In a weird way, it reminded him of what it was like to be swim team captain, when all his teammates looked up to him. He squeezed gently, watching the indentation his thumb made in the tomato's red skin. Suddenly, the tomato broke, splashing his Nike T-shirt.

"Yeah!" Lucas whooped, giving Vince a high five.

Emphasis: *high*.

"That was fucking beautiful," Lucas added, still entranced by the broken tomato.

Lisa stroked Rhys's tomato juice–covered arm. "It was like, you held the tomato, and then you just squeezed it and splat. And then it's like, broken. It's like a broken tomato. I could write a song about that," she mused. Rhys nodded thoughtfully, remembering Lisa playing the ukulele the first time they'd met.

"I could help you," Rhys offered. Lisa nodded eagerly.

"Let me get my ukulele. It's downstairs. Do you want to come with me?" Lisa batted her eyelashes, obviously flirting. Rhys considered. His brain felt all fuzzy. So Lisa wasn't Kelsey. She didn't wear cute, formfitting clothes or shave her legs or brush her hair or wear deodorant. But was there anything *wrong* with that?

Where to even begin?

swim team throwdown

Owen hurried up First Avenue, his hands jammed in the pockets of his slate-gray North Face fleece. It was Friday evening, and he had to go to the fucking swim team pasta party, where he was sure everyone would ignore him in favor of Hugh and his absurd captain hat. He hadn't talked to Kelsey since he'd run out of her apartment yesterday afternoon, ignoring her phone calls and texts like a pansy asshole. He wished there was someone he could talk to. His sisters were too nosy, and he certainly wouldn't talk about his relationship with his *mom*. He wanted to talk to a guy friend. Actually, the only person he wanted to talk to was . . . Rhys.

Stop being such a pussy, Carlyle, he whispered to himself, causing a guy pushing a shopping cart full of empty aluminum cans to gaze at him curiously. *Fuck*. He even looked crazy to the crazies. He turned at Ninetieth Street and headed toward the entrance of Normandie Courts, where Coach lived in a two-bedroom with an ex–swim team buddy of his from Stanford. Normandie Courts was a sprawling modern apartment complex on First Avenue that people jokingly called

Dormandie Courts, because so many kids moved there right after college.

Owen's stomach was in knots as he walked down the moldy-looking maroon carpeting toward the elevator bank. He'd so much rather be doing anything else. Maybe he'd take a page from Baby's book and just go to Barcelona. That'd be good.

"Hi, I'm going to 15A?" he told the burly security guard sitting behind a cracked laminate desk. He half-hoped the security guard would send him home or something, so he'd have an excuse not to attend.

"Go on up," the guard said, barely looking up.

Owen entered the elevator, feeling like he was going into a tank of sharks rather than a feel-good, pump-the-team up pasta dinner. He walked over to 15A and rang the dinky-looking doorbell, nervously adjusting his Nantucket Pirates swim cap.

"Captain, my captain!" Coach Siegel swung the door open, obviously more than a little drunk. Owen felt his stomach loosen up and he unballed his hands from the pockets of his stiff Lucky jeans. He'd been sort of worried he'd get another lecture from Coach, but that obviously wouldn't happen tonight. Owen sighed in relief.

"Don't look so sad!" Coach exclaimed, noticing Owen's expression. "Make yourself at home. There's brewskies in the fridge," he added with a wink.

"Thanks," Owen muttered and wandered into the tiny, cream-colored efficiency kitchen directly adjacent to the doorway. The sound of Dave Matthews emanated from the small Bose sound dock perched on the cracked Formica counter, as if Coach was trying to relive his Stanford house party days.

Just then, Hugh entered the kitchen. "Carlyle." He nodded stiffly.

"Hi." Owen smiled awkwardly and busied himself pulling beers from the fridge. "Need anything?"

"I'll get it myself. I don't need anything from you," Hugh said, brushing past Owen to grab beers from the fridge.

Owen hastily exited the kitchen, Bud Light in hand. He used the bottom of his thin gray T-shirt to unscrew the cap of his beer, then wandered into the tiny living room.

Around him, guys were chugging Buds and halfheartedly watching a baseball game playing on the forty-two-inch flat screen. A small group of freshmen were huddled in awe around a Playboy *Centerfolds of the Ages* book, which Chadwick held open on his lap like a storybook. Owen perched dubiously on a well-used Barcalounger that looked like it had been rescued from the side of the street. Propped next to it was a three-foot-tall blow-up bottle of Bud Light.

Classy.

"Carlyle!" Coach yelled from across the room, his hand held up in greeting.

"One sec!" Owen called. He wasn't sure where he could hide in a tiny apartment, but he didn't feel like chatting right now. He wandered over to the bathroom. The door was locked.

"May be a while!" Owen recognized Hugh's voice. Great. He didn't even want to know what Hugh was doing in there. He turned and looked out the window. It faced onto row after row of boring-looking apartment complexes. He sighed in frustration.

"It's a tough life." Owen glanced over at the overweight guy standing next to him, immediately recognizing him as Coach's roommate, Mike. Coach often invoked him as a cautionary tale to his St. Jude's swimmers: Mike had been a star swimmer at Stanford, then had gotten involved with a high-maintenance girlfriend, quit swimming, and dropped out of college to follow her to grad school in New York, where he'd promptly been dumped, begun working at Red Lobster in Times Square, and gained seventy-five pounds.

"Yeah," Owen grunted, edging away as if Mike's loser vibes were contagious.

"But as long as you have friends, that's what counts." As if to prove his point, he burped beerily. Owen nodded, pretending to be supremely interested in something happening out the window so he wouldn't have to talk to Mike. Somewhere out there, he knew, Rhys was alone and probably lonely. Owen needed to apologize. A girl was *never* worth it. Why hadn't he realized that before?

"I've gotta go, man," he mumbled to Mike. He set his Bud Light down on the linoleum floor, hurried out the door, and down the hall. They'd never miss him.

In the elevator, a group of guys all wearing pink Abercrombie polo shirts and dorky-looking khakis were toasting each other with ill-concealed forties they'd duct-taped to their hands. They were playing Edward Fortyhands, where you couldn't use your hands until you'd finished the forties attached to them. By the end, you were a drunk, stupid mess, and you couldn't even untape the bottles yourself—someone else had to. But that was exactly the point. It was about teamwork. The sight of them almost made Owen want to cry for the friendships he'd lost.

Once he got to the corner, Owen stuck his hand out, trying to hail a cab. All the cabs streaming down First were taken, obviously transporting uptowners to parties and bars downtown. Frustrated, Owen glanced down at his scuffed Stan Smith sneakers. He'd just have to run.

★ ★ ★

Finally, he reached Rhys's town house. He could hear music thumping from outside. Were his parents throwing a party or something? Owen pressed his finger firmly on the doorbell.

"Hey man!" A lanky guy with dreadlocks opened the door and smiled widely at him.

"Um, hi." Owen paused, confused. He glanced at the brass numbers attached to the door. Eighty-seven. This was definitely the right house. "Um, is Rhys home?"

"Rhys?" The guy shook his head in confusion and wandered away, leaving the door wide open. Shrugging, Owen followed him inside.

"Rhys?" he called. His voice echoed off the dark oak paneling of the foyer. Weird music was emanating from downstairs. He edged his way around the foyer and into the living room and ran down the stairs two at a time, opening the door into the indoor pool area.

Owen was always impressed with the pool in the Sterlings' basement. While his grandmother's town house had a pool, it was three feet deep and fifteen feet wide. Rhys's pool was twenty-five yards long and five feet deep, tiled with hand-painted Italian panels of starfish, octopus, and kelp. Not that it looked too impressive now. The air seemed foggier than usual, and random kids were lounging on the deck in various states of undress. One guy was maniacally throwing tomatoes into the water as if he were playing some sort of game only he knew the rules to. Phish was blaring through the sound system. What was going on? Owen's eyes finally landed on Rhys, lying on a float in the center of the pool.

"Hey man! You made it!" The guy who'd let Owen in smiled enthusiastically from the shallow end of the pool. "Coming in?" he asked.

"Rhys?" Owen called, ignoring the random kid. Who *were* these people? And why was Rhys hanging out with them? "Rhys?" Owen called again, his voice tinged with desperation.

"Why the fuck are you here?" Rhys yelled back, not bothering to move from his float.

"Can we talk?" Owen called tentatively, still standing at the edge of the pool. He ducked to avoid a tomato, thrown at close range by the dreadlocked kid sitting on a lounge chair. What the hell? Why was Rhys hanging out with losers like this? It was as if he had gotten a brain transplant or something.

"Please, can you talk to me?" Owen yelled again. He knew he sounded like he was begging. But he didn't care.

"We *are* talking!" Rhys shouted back. Owen realized that everyone was completely quiet. Thinking quickly, he pulled off his shirt and dove into the water, swimming over to Rhys.

"What's going on?" He shook out his hair and firmly held on to the edge of Rhys's yellow float.

"Why are you here?" Rhys countered. He shook his head, annoyed. "You ruined my life. It's good now. See. These people are good people."

Whatever you say.

"Okay—fine," Owen said awkwardly, not wanting to start a fight. "I know you hate me right now. But it's just—come back to the team. I'll quit. They want *you* as captain, not me," Owen said simply, letting go of the float and attempting to stand up in the water. His right foot landed on something squishy. *Ugh.* He looked down and saw a waterlogged tomato, splatted against one of the starfish designs. It looked like the starfish had been murdered.

Rhys leaned back on the float, as if he hadn't heard Owen. Owen sniffed the air. It definitely didn't smell like chlorine.

"Who are these people? Are you smoking *pot*?" Owen whispered.

"They're my *friends*," Rhys said icily. He looked spacey and out of it. Owen didn't know what to do. "Just . . . leave me alone. You've helped me enough," he spat, paddling his float away from Owen.

"Cannonball!" On the other side of the pool, the dreadlocked guy jumped into the water.

"Yeah!" Rhys yelled happily.

"*No!*" Owen yelled forcefully, surprising himself.

"Dude, chill out!" The dreadlocked dude doggy-paddled over to Owen. "Hey man, it doesn't seem like you're adding positive energy to the party. Rhys is just chillin'. What'd he do to you?" he asked curiously.

"Nothing," Owen responded simply. Rhys *hadn't* done anything. He'd been the only best friend Owen had ever had, until Owen had completely betrayed him. "If you guys are his friends . . . I guess everything is cool," he said slowly. Owen shook his head and looked one last time at Rhys.

"Dude, this isn't you," he hissed quietly to Rhys.

Rhys laughed bitterly as he glanced toward Owen. Owen's face looked pale and drawn.

"*You're* going to tell me who I am?" Of course Owen was being judgmental. He couldn't see his friends for who they were: people who actually cared about him.

"Actually, yeah," Owen said seriously. "Look, I know we might never be friends again. But just so you know, you were the best buddy I've ever had. And I miss you. And all the swim team guys do, too. Please come back. Our meet is against Unity tomorrow at ten. And honestly . . . you belong in the St. Jude's pool, as captain. Not here, doing whatever it is you're doing with these people." Owen shrugged.

"Thanks," Rhys spit sarcastically. Why should he care about a stupid swim meet? He had better things to do.

Like smoke up, play the ukulele with hairy-legged girls, and juggle tomatoes, obviously.

Just then, Lucas paddled over. One of his hands was held high in the air, clearly on a mission to get a joint over to Rhys.

"Rhys!" Lucas called joyfully. "Dude, here's a little special delivery." He passed the joint to Rhys.

Rhys took the joint and inhaled, wanting to blow the smoke straight in Owen's face. He didn't need him to tell him what to do. He was *fine*.

Owen shook his head. This was pointless. He swam to the side of the pool and pulled himself out. The worst part was, he'd caused this mess. And there was nothing he could do about it. He pulled on his shirt, not caring that it would get soaked, walked up the stairs, and firmly closed the front door.

j's unveiling

"Jack, over here!"

Jack giddily whirled around on the red carpet as flashbulbs went off. Dick's Stepford-wife publicity team had gone all out on the launch party for the Cashman Lofts. The entire West Broadway block occupied by the lofts had been blocked off with blue police barricades, while a red carpet and spotlights outside the door made the event seem more like a movie premiere than a building opening. The guest list was similarly glamorous, with an A-list guest list mixing with real estate and media types. Further up on the carpet, Jack could see Leonardo DiCaprio and some model-y girl, but none of the photographers seemed to care. Instead, they were all clamoring around *her*.

Jack shivered, her backless white Christian Dior gown not entirely appropriate for October weather.

"Ready, princess?" Dick Cashman lumbered easily onto the red carpet from a Lincoln Town Car. He wore his trademark leather cowboy hat, but had added a festive red bow around the brim. Tatyana strode behind him, wearing a gold Chanel dress that would have shown an obscene amount of cleavage had she not been carrying one of her puggles—Nemo or Memo or what-ever its name was—close to her chest. The terrified pet looked like it wanted to crawl *into* her cleavage, rather than deal with the super-bright flashbulbs.

"Aw, I should help my mom," J.P., looking handsome in a crisp charcoal suit, said, gesturing to Tatyana desperately trying to keep control of her dog. Jack nodded, not really paying atten-tion.

"All righty, then, we're in this together," Dick Cashman boomed, putting a hand around Jack's waist and pulling her close to him. Suddenly, flashbulbs began working overtime.

"Dick and Jack!" one pimply-faced photographer yelled from behind a police barricade. Dick whirled around and smiled. Jack cringed inwardly. Together, their names sounded like the title of some sort of perverted learn-to-read book.

Fun with Dick and Jack?

Where the fuck was her actual boyfriend? She didn't want to be rude or anything, but she'd much rather be photographed on the arm of J.P. than on the arm of his fat, red, totally embarrass-ing aw-shucks dad.

"We'll get some shots of you and J.P.," Dick boomed, as if reading her mind. "And now, all I want you kids to do at this little hoedown is have fun. And that's an order." Dick Cash-man practically pushed her through the doors of the building, and Jack took a deep breath. The lobby of the lofts was sump-tuously decorated like a rain forest, complete with twisted vines snaking from spindly tree to spindly tree, leopard-print ottomans, and a leaf-patterned carpet. It could have looked like a hokey theme restaurant, but instead it really did feel like a jungle oasis.

Jack hurriedly grabbed a glass of champagne from a passing waiter and took a deep gulp. There. That was better.

"Hey." Jack smiled in relief to see J.P. standing in front of her, holding two glasses of champagne. "Oh, you already have a drink," he noted.

"I'll take another." Jack smiled coquettishly. "After all, we have a lot to celebrate!" She clinked her glass against his. His dark brown hair was combed over to the side and he wore a classic Armani suit with an emerald green tie that matched the jungle décor without being too obvious.

"I grabbed us a table," J.P. said, slipping his hand through hers and escorting her through the arch-ceilinged lobby. "You look beautiful tonight."

"Thanks," Jack replied. She squeezed his hand hard. He smelled like John Varvatos Vintage cologne and suddenly, she wanted to go back upstairs to the penthouse—now. "Hey, I was thinking—" Jack whispered in J.P.'s ear.

"Jack, darling!" Beatrice Morris swooped down and planted a kiss on Jack's freckled cheek. Beatrice was Jiffy Bennett's thirty-two-year-old, three-times-married sister. She'd been a regular on the social circuit since she was sixteen and had gotten married for the first time at nineteen. Next to her now was a much older man, dressed in an all-white suit, clinging to the crook of her alarmingly skinny elbow.

"Nice to see you," Jack responded shortly. The last time she'd seen Beatrice, she'd been married to a man who was ten years younger. Clearly, now she was swinging in the opposite direction.

Covering all the bases.

"This is my fiancé, Deptford Morris," she cooed. The old man extended a shaky hand to Jack.

"Nice to meet you," Jack said quickly, shaking his clammy hand.

"And you're doing very well, I can tell!" Beatrice leaned in conspiratorially. "Real estate men are the best. I wish I'd learned that earlier," she whispered, moving in so close that Jack felt suffocated by the smell of her Creed Royal perfume. Jack backed away, nearly stepping on Beatrice's red Prada dress.

"Anyway, you need to teach Jiffy a thing or two. She needs a man to take care of her. That girl has no common sense," Beatrice shook her head fondly. Jack narrowed her eyes. Was Jiffy's skanky sister insinuating she was choosing men for their money?

"J.P.'s been my boyfriend for years," she clarified firmly.

"Then so much the better, darling!" Beatrice said easily. "We're going to go to the bar. Deptford gets cranky if we get home past ten." A shadow of a frown crossed Beatrice's face, only to be replaced by a fake-looking smile as she swanned off.

"So, when do you think we can go upstairs?" Jack asked, arching an eyebrow at J.P.

"There you kids are!" Candice interrupted, grabbing both of their elbows and ushering them over to a VIP section that was cordoned off by a velvet rope and surrounded by two poster-size photographs of Jack. They were shots that hadn't been used in the campaign yet, of her wearing an emerald-green Prada raincoat and frolicking in one of the fountains flanking the Cashman Lofts courtyard. It didn't look like Jack was wearing anything under the coat. It had seemed cool at the time, but looking at the photos in the dim light of the lobby, they almost looked trashy, like Jack was some pervy flasher. She turned away. Luckily, right behind her was a waiter bearing champagne and green-colored cocktails. She grabbed one of each.

Bottoms up!

"We have some interviews for you kids to do with press. We're setting it up in the penthouse, out of the way of this circus. We're sort of seeing you as the new Donald Trump and Ivana," Candice cooed, playing with Jack's auburn hair.

Jack stiffened. They were doing interviews in her *apartment*?

"In the glamour years, of course. Pre-1985," Jeannette clarified, typing furiously on her BlackBerry as if to make a note of that. Jack resisted the urge to pour the rest of her champagne down Candice's tight black silk Dior blouse. What if she didn't *want* to be the next Ivana Trump? Wasn't Ivana Trump *tacky*?

And aren't J.P.'s parents *already* the new Donald and Ivana?

"Come," Candice urged. Jack grabbed another glass of champagne. She was going to need it.

Better take the whole bottle.

beautiful enemies

"Thanks." Avery attempted to gracefully exit the Lincoln Town Car onto the red carpet that lined the sidewalk outside the Cashman Lofts on Friday night. Her heart skipped a beat as James steadied her elbow while she found her footing in her killer black satin peep-toe Prada pumps, which she'd paired with a black lace Diane von Furstenberg dress. She smiled as she noticed the rows of photographers, furiously taking pictures of all the party attendees. When she'd heard about the party, she'd imagined it would be filled mostly with no-name media and real estate types, but it seemed everyone in New York City—not to mention half of Hollywood—was here. Before tonight, the closest she'd come to an honest-to-God red carpet was the annual lobster cookout sponsored by the Nantucket Fire Department. This was a billion times better. She flashed a megawatt smile at James.

"James!" Gemma, who Avery knew was working the party, ran up to them from the other end of the red carpet. She wore boring black pants and a black blouse with a clunky headset behind her ears. Vines were braided into her hair, a lame attempt at matching the party's jungle theme.

"Hi Gemma!" Avery air-kissed Gemma's pale cheek, as if she were thrilled to see her. "How's work?" she added bitchily.

"Here are your press credentials," Gemma handed them two dorky name badges. "Ticky wants you to do some interviews with Jack Laurent. She just got in." Gemma rolled her eyes, clearly hating her role as messenger. Avery grinned. Who was the intern now?

Technically, still her?

"Lovely, thank you." James kissed Gemma on the cheek. "Maybe we'll bring you some champagne. If you're good!" he said, smiling flirtatiously at Gemma.

What? Avery frowned. Was James flirting with Gemma?

They walked through the lofts lobby, skirting the vines hanging from the ceiling and the leopard- and zebra-print sofas placed around the room. Performers dressed in giraffe and zebra costumes walked around, looking lost among the dozens of couture-clad guests milling about the lobby-turned-jungle-oasis.

"I want you to be my eyes and ears," James said, leaning toward Avery's ear, suddenly all business. "Things can always get spectacularly cocked up at parties, if you know what I mean." Avery nodded, even though she had no idea what he was talking about. *Cocked up?* Did something get lost in translation?

Or is someone thinking below the belt?

"Follow Jack and see what she does, who she says things to, and where she goes post-party. Follow her to the loo. Be as friendly and natural as possible. You want it so when she's talking, it's like she's talking to herself. Get inside her brain. Consider this your crash course in journalism, kid," James instructed.

"Here you go." He handed Avery a glass of champagne taken from a passing waiter. "Now, be a good girl and do me proud. I have to do the usual cocktail party loop. Tragic, really." James shook his head.

"Sure," Avery said numbly. Why didn't he want to hang out with *her*? And was she really expected to follow Jack Laurent around? The room was so crowded she doubted she'd even *find* her.

"Okay, babe. You'll be okay?" James asked. But he was already swaggering through the crowd, pushing past people to try to get to the VIP room on the side of the lobby.

"Organic lamb burger?" A tuxedoed waiter held up a silver platter to Avery's nose. She grabbed one of the tiny burgers and unhappily took a bite. Suddenly James seemed less like an attentive date and more like a self-centered reporter using her for *his* story.

"Avery!" Ticky strode up on her infamous five-inch sparkly Miu Miu heels, leaving a trail of sequins in her wake. Only Ticky could get away with wearing the same pair of shoes so often, because she wore them with an *I don't give a fuck* attitude, like she was so fabulous *of course* only sparkly shoes would do.

Of course.

She was clinging to the hand of a man who was six inches shorter and probably twenty years younger. He had neatly groomed yellow-white hair and wore a crisp white suit that was cut to fit his diminutive frame. "Avery, darling, this is Bailey Winter, the designer. He agreed to follow this old battleship around all night!" Ticky exclaimed.

"Darling, there's no one else I'd *rather* follow!" Bailey Winter protested, waving a hand in the air.

Avery smiled uncertainly. She knew that Bailey Winter was an important fashion designer and normally, she'd have been thrilled to meet him. But now that she'd been abandoned by James, she felt shy, like Ticky might decide on the spot that she'd been wrong about assigning her the story: that she was simply not *Metropolitan* material.

"Hi," she finally mustered. She noticed McKenna trailing behind the two of them, carrying Ticky's silver Prada clutch in one hand and Bailey Winter's huge black Prada satchel over her shoulder. She had the same dorky-looking walkie-talkie as Gemma.

"You're all alone!" Ticky noticed, leaning in to air-kiss Avery. Ticky smelled like cigarettes, scotch, and those hard butterscotch candies Avery's grandmother always used to eat.

"Yes, that's so sad, Avery. At least you found the food!" McKenna smiled fakely. Avery glowered. Of course McKenna had to see her standing around like a friendless loser, feeding her sorrows with organic calories.

"I'm actually here with James. He and I are just . . . covering different people," Avery lied.

"Pshaw!" Ticky waved her red-manicured hand wildly in the air. Her hair didn't move from its lacquered bouffant, the same style Avery's grandmother used to wear to special events.

Noting something was wrong, Ticky rested a bony hand on Avery's bare shoulder. "You've learned the hard way, darling. James is a fantastic reporter, but he's a fucking celebrosexual. You can't take him anywhere." Ticky rolled her heavily made-up eyes. "So forget whatever orders James gave you and just have fun tonight. Circulate! Mingle! Your job is to be the fabulous face of *Metropolitan*. Someone has to be. No matter how many refreshers I've gotten from Dr. Antell, my face won't cut it anymore," Ticky added ruefully.

"Thanks," Avery said numbly.

"Now, I have to make sure everyone knows I'm here and not dead yet."

"My dear, your life has only just begun!" Bailey Winter exclaimed, leading Ticky over to the bar.

"Have fun!" Ticky commanded again, looking over her shoulder before she disappeared into the crowd.

Avery nodded, then moved safely out of Ticky's view. She navigated her way past the spindly, weird-looking trees set up for the occasion and toward an exit sign. She just needed some air.

"Did you want to see the penthouse?" A blond girl standing near the elevators asked, clearly noting the dorky press badge she and James had been given at the door.

"Sure," Avery agreed curiously. Wasn't the penthouse where Jack was living?

"Great," the girl enthused, holding the elevator door open for Avery. "You can just go up. I believe Jack Laurent is there giving interviews."

"Perfect," Avery murmured, watching the girl press *P*. So she was going to find Jack after all.

The elevator door opened into a cavernous, all-white and gray loft space. Cameras were set up in one corner. Jack and J.P. were obviously being interviewed. J.P. was gesticulating wildly, looking like he was having the time of his life. Jack was smiling, but something seemed off.

"You're press?" A woman placed a manicured hand on Avery's shoulder.

"Yeah. I mean, yes. From *Metropolitan*," Avery said, appraising the skinny, black-clad woman in front of her. The woman's face broke into a smile.

"Oh, *Metropolitan*. Lovely. I'm Jeannette. With the lofts. I suppose you want to speak to Jack and J.P.?"

"Um, no. I mean, it looks like they're busy," Avery said. Suddenly, coming up here seemed like a stupid idea. She *really* didn't want to talk to Jack one-on-one.

Jeannette regarded her curiously. "Nonsense. I want them to speak to *Metropolitan*. They're just finishing up a *Harper's* interview now, but I'll come fetch you when they're done. Perhaps you'd like to take a peek around? The views from the terrace are quite lovely," Jeannette said, grabbing the crook of her arm and pulling her toward the terrace.

Outside, Avery gazed up at the larger-than-life billboard of Jack. In the photograph, she looked beautiful and sweet, a girl who'd never make someone's life a living hell just because she could.

"Lovely, isn't she?" Jeannette said, following Avery's gaze. "I'll see if they're through. In the meantime, is there anything I can get you?"

Avery shook her head, transfixed by the billboard. Even though it was sort of her job and the reason she was here, she still couldn't quite believe she'd be forced to *interview* Jack.

"Avery."

Avery whirled around and saw Jack, standing alone by the terrace door, her auburn hair hanging loose around her shoulders. "Hi, Jack," Avery said stiffly.

"Well, let's get this over with. I can't believe they're making me do an interview with an *intern*," Jack sniffed. She thought she'd seen Avery and some older guy at the bar, but had immediately dismissed it. Because why the fuck would Avery Carlyle be at the Cashman Lofts launch party, an event so exclusive even *she* couldn't get any of her friends in? And now, it turned out that Avery was *interviewing* her.

"I'm glad we have the chance to talk," Avery began, hating how fake she sounded. She remembered what James had said, about cornering Jack. Even though he was rude and self-obsessed, now was the time to *really* get some good quotes and impress the hell out of him and Ticky. "I don't know how you do these things all the time without just freaking out," she added, hoping the sympathy route would get Jack to open up. "I would."

"It's not that hard." Jack rolled her eyes. Was Avery for real? And what could Avery *possibly* have to freak out about? "Why aren't you with your boyfriend?" she asked, remembering the older dude she'd seen with Avery.

"I don't have a boyfriend," Avery replied smoothly. She cringed as she said it. "Why aren't you out here with *your* boyfriend?" Avery countered.

"I need a minute without him," Jack said tightly. She took a drag of her cigarette. "Want a smoke?" She pulled a pack of Merits from her gold quilted Louis Vuitton purse, knowing she'd say no. That was the thing. Avery wouldn't be so goddamn annoying if she weren't so *good*. Hopefully the threat of carcinogens would make the pure-lunged Avery leave her alone.

"Sure." Avery held out her hand and smiled. Jack raised an eyebrow. Avery certainly was full of surprises. Jack carefully lit the cigarette with her own and passed it over to Avery.

Just then, Jeannette opened the door of the terrace. "We've

got some other press who wants to speak with you. Do you think you'll be a while?" Jeannette asked, wrinkling her nose at Jack and Avery's cigarettes.

"No," Avery said.

"Yes," Jack overrode her. "We haven't even started yet."

Avery narrowed her eyes. Was Jack asking for *more* time with her?

"Okay." Jeannette's lips were pursed in disapproval.

"These interviews are kind of lame. No offense," Jack sighed after Jeanette had left. "I really don't feel like doing any more."

"It's fine. I don't really know what I'm doing," Avery confessed.

"I wish I did." Jack shrugged, taking another drag. "Also, you're kind of lucky you don't have a boyfriend." She remembered back when she could flirt with whomever she wanted.

For the one week she was single?

"What do you mean?" Avery inhaled, then began to cough, finally dropping the cigarette on the slate floor and stomping it with the toe of her Prada pump. She was all for being friendly with Jack to make her spill, but she didn't want to sacrifice her lungs for it.

"I don't smoke." She smiled and shrugged.

"I shouldn't." Jack frowned. "I've just been stressed out this week," she added, lighting up another cigarette.

"Why?" The question came out sounding like a complaint. It was hard to feel sorry for Jack. After all, she was an almost professional ballerina, had a super-hot, perfect boyfriend, and a fledgling modeling career. What could she possibly have to stress about? Which designer sample dress to wear every night?

"This whole Cashman Lofts thing is just weird. I mean, I love the apartment, but it sort of feels like I'm married to J.P."

A frown crossed Jack's face and Avery nodded sympathetically, even though she didn't understand the problem with that.

"Please don't use that in an interview. I mean, it's just that everything's happening really fast," Jack clarified, almost as if she were talking to herself. It was sort of nice to let someone know what she was thinking. If she'd told this to Genevieve or Jiffy, they'd think she was crazy. And maybe she was. Who wouldn't love a rent-free apartment, a loving boyfriend, and millions of invites to the hottest parties in town?

"I don't know what the fuck I'm supposed to be doing," Jack added. "I mean, my mom is this super-crazy dramatic French ex-ballerina who moved to Paris this past week to be on a soap opera. And I can't even deal with that because I'm so busy dealing with a dog that eats my shoes and a boyfriend who never wants to leave the house and his crazy, no-boundaries parents and just . . . all of this!" she wailed, then began laughing. Her life sounded so ridiculous, it was kind of hard not to.

"That's not bad. All parents are embarrassing. I mean, my mom's a crazy artist who collects glass octopus sculptures," Avery offered.

"I know." Jack nodded, remembering the absurd dinner party she'd gone to at the Carlyles', where Avery's mom had been raving about her octopuses. Suddenly, they both started laughing. It was almost like they were having *fun*. Next thing she knew, she'd be telling Avery she was a virgin.

Maybe they could start a club!

"But you're still living by yourself in an awesome apartment," Avery reminded her, trying to get back into interview mode. She had to stay on track. Still, she couldn't help thinking of some of the sentences from James's article. Jack might be self-centered and competitive, but she *definitely* wasn't sleeping with her boyfriend's dad. Avery felt the champagne swirl in her empty stomach. But what could she do about it?

"An awesome apartment that's like *The Situation Room* right now. I mean, honestly, it's just a billboard." Jack glanced up at her larger-than-life image. "What you're doing seems cool, though. As long as you don't write anything bad about me," Jack laughed uncertainly.

"Don't worry," Avery said faintly, even though she felt like she could throw up right now. Jack had no idea just how bad the article would be.

"I'd understand if you did. Look, I know I was kind of a bitch. That's the way I am." Jack shrugged, then stamped out her cigarette. "But I'm sorry." She looked straight ahead into the night air.

"Thanks," Avery said, suddenly shivering. It wasn't as if Jack had really *chosen* to be on the billboard . . . and now, everyone in New York was going to think she'd slept her way to a free apartment. With her boyfriend's *dad*, no less. Suddenly James, for all his talk of journalistic excellence, was seeming like the true villain, while Jack was . . . well, no angel. But also not as evil as Avery had made her out to be.

"Do you want to get out of here?" Jack asked shyly. "We can pretend we're doing an in-depth interview. If we're together, no one can bitch at us for not doing whatever the fuck we're supposed to be doing. And I *really* need another drink." Jack offered a tentative smile.

Avery nodded. It actually sounded like the best plan she'd heard all night.

"Let's do it!" Jack turned on her heel and Avery followed behind her. After a few glasses of champagne, she could just forget all about James and Gemma and Ticky and the whole *Metropolitan* article.

Because when you forget about something, it automatically disappears.

cleaning out my closet

"Baby?" Edie's voice echoed through the hallway on Friday night.

"Yeah?" Baby called, deftly stepping over their black cat, Rothko. She was deep inside her closet, not even knowing how to begin to follow Lynn's orders. Vintage dresses were puddled in heaps on top of each other. Cardboard boxes she hadn't bothered opening since they'd moved from Nantucket were precariously stacked against the back wall. Photos were scattered on the hardwood floor.

"What are you doing?" Edie asked, stepping into the walk-in closet. "Oh!" She bent down and picked up a mustard yellow wool poncho off the floor. "This was mine!" she exclaimed tenderly, her voice muffled as she pulled it over her blond-bobbed head and modeled it for her Baby. "What do you think?"

Baby critically appraised her middle-aged mom. Rather than making her appear shapeless, it actually accentuated Edie's rail-thin frame and made her look almost cool.

Relatively speaking, obviously.

"Nice, Mom," Baby said. "You want it back?"

"No." Edie shook her head. "This was from the year I worked on an organic farm in Vermont. It was a few years before you three were born. Too many memories." Edie shrugged and pulled it off, shaking her head as if to get rid of any negative associations.

"Really?" Baby asked, surprised. It sounded like Edie had been following Lynn's advice, not to hang on to anything that caused her pain. Was it really just common sense?

"Yeah. It just doesn't work for me," Edie said, ruffling her daughter's hair. "Anyway, I know your brother and sister are out, so I'm just letting you know I'm heading out as well. I'm meeting Remington," she added conspiratorially. "Will you be all right by yourself? You've seemed distracted lately. I've been meaning to ask you about it, but I know that you like to find your own answers. To stumble on the path. You're a lot like me," Edie added fondly.

"I'm okay," Baby said, meaning it. Or at least, she knew she'd be okay, soon enough. But she had to be the one to work through her problems—no therapist held the key. "But thanks, Mom." Baby smiled. She glanced at her closet with renewed vigor, her eyes falling on the way too long Citizen jeans she'd stolen from Avery last year. She might as well give those back.

"Good." Edie smiled and glided out of the room. "Don't wait up for me!"

Baby sat down on the closet floor and pulled a box toward her. She opened the flaps and peered inside. There were dozens of old 45 records, a gift from her eighth-grade boyfriend, even though neither of them had had record players. *Those* could definitely go. Underneath the records was a marble-bound composition book. Baby quickly riffled through the pages. It was a scrapbook filled with photos, written-out lyrics, and ticket stubs that she'd made as a Valentine's present for Tom, who had, in typical stoner style, never gotten around to taking it home. She wrinkled her nose. *That* could definitely go, too.

Rothko stepped on Baby's lap, swiping his paw at a piece of white gauzy material above him.

"You helping?" Baby asked in a singsongy voice, burying her face in the cat's soft fur. She pulled down the material he'd been swiping at. It was a beautiful white Rodarte dress with flowers hand sewn along the bodice. It was the dress she'd worn at the swim team benefit, the night she'd broken up with J.P. His mother had picked it out for her and while it was beautiful, Baby had spent the whole dance feeling awkward and stifled.

Definitively, she threw it into the donation pile. It was beautiful, and hopefully for someone else, it would have only good associations. But it wasn't for her. Rothko meowed indignantly, stalked over to the dress, and lay down on it.

"You can have it." Baby shrugged and smiled, not even feeling silly for talking to the cat. Instead, she felt a wave of relief flood through her. Seeing the pile forming on the "no" side of the floor reminded her that she wasn't dating a stoner, or a preppy buttoned-up mogul in training. She was dating . . . *herself*. Because really, who was more important to please than that?

Aye-aye, sister!

gossipgirl.net

Disclaimer: All the real names of places, people, and events have been altered or abbreviated to protect the innocent. Namely, me.

| topics | sightings | your e-mail | post a question |

hey people!

party patrol news flash

We interrupt your regularly scheduled partying to bring you this bulletin: A certain auburn-haired socialite and the star of tonight's show is *gone*. Don't put out the Amber alert or anything—I think we can safely say she left willingly. But a little after midnight, the face of the green movement was nowhere to be found. Most curious was her partner in crime: girl reporter **A**, known to be **J**'s frenemy, seems to be missing, too. Hmmm. Caviar-toast points and a jungle theme just weren't cutting it for **J**? It's my party and I'll ditch if I want to?

So I guess it's official, then: Leaving early is the new staying out all night. Unless you want to be seen as a friendless loser who has nowhere else to go, make sure you leave a party before the witching hour—when the bartenders stops serving drinks, girls are found not so subtly taking naps on the furniture in the ladies' lounge, and the bouncer is kicking people out instead of letting them in. Remember, it's not a competition, and you're not winning points for being the last one tottering around in your Manolos.

sleeping over

Of course, this time of night is when the afterparties start. If you're hosting, proceed with caution. Sooner or later, your guests are going to fall asleep—most likely with each other. And the morning-after drama is not for the faint of heart.

So where does that leave you? You could be like some and skip the party to clean out your closet. At least you'll be popular with your maid. Or you could host a hippie hempfest at your town house, like some others. Whatever you're doing—whether you're in the VIP room, knee-deep in couture, or getting wasted with your new BFF—have fun tonight! Or at least, with what's left of it. There are about five hours till sunrise, which is when even I hang up my dancing shoes. . . .

sightings

B outside her apartment building, throwing away armfuls of clothing and other trinkets. Spring cleaning in October? . . . **A** and **J** drinking five-dollar pitchers of Bud Light at some divey bar on Lispenard Street, around the corner from the Cashman Lofts—did the party change location? **J** stumbling into a cab, stumbling back into the lofts, then stumbling into an elevator with **J.P.**—and an army of photogs. Seems like one couple won't be getting very much sleep . . . and not for the reason they'd hoped. **O** getting takeout at some Chinese joint on third, then hurrying home—solo. What a shame, especially since we *all* know what an aphrodisiac greasy Chinese food can be. **R** paying some pizza guy outside his apartment. I know prices have gone up, but the cash he slipped him seemed to more than cover a couple pies.

your e-mail

Dear Gossip Girl,
You're cute. Tell you what. Meet me at the Waverly, 8 p.m., Monday. I'm gonna make you a star, kiddo.
—sunglassesatnight

a: Dear SatN,

Thanks for the invite, but I'm pretty content with my current star wattage.

—GG

q: Dear Gossip Girl,

I'm a guidance counselor at Harrington, a private, independent, all-boys boarding school in the UK. I received an application from one young man's parents. He goes to an excellent school in Manhattan and has a stellar academic record. That's all well and good, but we do like to get a sense of our boys through their peers so we'll know if they'll be a good fit into our community. If you can vouch for him, then we'll let him in immediately. Cheerio!

—RugbyandCrew

a: Dear Rugby,

Sadly, I don't think this bloke will be able to be pulled away from New York—or his mother's greenhouse—any time soon. The climate of the UK isn't so good for the type of growth he wishes to do. Although he certainly gets along with diverse groups!

—Gossip Girl

All right. Back to the afterparty.

You know you love me.

gossip girl

r gets clean

"Cuddle party, man!"

Rhys woke up on Saturday morning to something thudding against his chest. What the fuck? He'd just been having a dream that he was living in the bakery section of Zabar's, in a self-constructed hut of baguettes. It was a pretty good dream actually. Now he opened one eye to a brilliant blue sky, with clouds floating above him. Where the *fuck* was he?

Hint: not an Upper West Side food emporium.

"You're awake!" a gleeful voice called. Suddenly, the tanned face of Lucas appeared above him, grinning.

"Guh," Rhys burbled. It was too hard to actually form any words. He opened one eye again. His eyes felt weird and crusted together. Lucas was standing above him, clad in one of Rhys's dad's kilts, sans shirt. He was holding what Rhys recognized as his parents' custom-made sheets from the Monogrammed Linen Shop in London above his head like a tent.

"Come on, feel the love, brother!" a female voice slurred in a half-stoned, half-drunk monotone. Rhys suddenly noticed a strange weight on his arm. He looked over to see Lisa slung across it, her hairy armpit raised to the sun as if in salutation.

That'll wake you up in the morning.

Rhys hurriedly pushed himself up into a standing position. He felt seasick, like the time he and his parents had spent a month cruising on the Aegean, then stopped abruptly on some random island. As soon as he'd stepped ashore, he'd thrown up, even though he'd never once felt sick on the boat.

"You don't look so good," Lucas said in concern. "You need a bowl." He pulled his pipe out of the back pocket of his cargo shorts.

"No!" Rhys yelled, practically ready to hurl as he stood up. Lucas shrugged, then lay in the spot Rhys had been, snuggling next to Lisa. Lucas closed his eyes and immediately seemed to fall asleep. Rhys glanced wildly around, feeling his heart beat faster and faster. What the fuck had *happened* last night? He looked around the terrace. There was a pyramid constructed out of empty Tecate cans, and, inexplicably, the Italian greyhound sculpture from downstairs.

"What did we do?" Rhys mumbled weakly, though it wasn't like anyone was listening. He wobbled down the narrow staircase from the terrace to the rest of the house. Maybe they'd just spent the whole time on the terrace. Maybe it wasn't too bad.

Or maybe it's a million times worse.

"What's going on?" Rhys called tentatively, walking into the kitchen. Tins of caviar were open and strewn across the Italian marble island in the center of the room.

"Dude, I think your fridge is broken. The milk tastes funky." Vince shook his head sadly, pulling away from the refrigerator. Rhys looked down and realized half the hardwood floor was covered with four inches of water.

"Man, that party rocked," Vince continued, seemingly unaware water was pooled up to his ankles. Rhys nodded tightly. As long as the damage was confined to the kitchen, it wasn't *that* bad.

"Dude, you're such a fucking good swimmer. You were tearing it up on the float last night."

Sitting on the floor, among the corgis' food bowls, was a kid Rhys had never even seen. He was stacking a pile of scones into a tower, furrowing his brow in consternation. Rhys gripped the countertop for support. All of a sudden, images from last night flashed through his mind. Bobbing for his mom's tomatoes in the pool. Making bongs out of the tomatoes. Smoking up. Sharing a sloppy kiss with Lisa on the balcony. Raiding the kitchen cabinet and the wine cellar. Oh no.

"I'm gonna be sick," Rhys announced, turning and bolting to the bathroom. Inside, tomato juice stained the delicate rose-printed wallpaper. A guy and a girl were both sleeping peacefully in the tub, the guy holding a bong protectively against his chest like a long-lost friend.

"Out!" Rhys yelled. Even yelling hurt. All he wanted to do was take a long shower and hope this was a long, weird, trippy nightmare that would soon be over.

The phone rang.

"'Lo?" Rhys could hear Vince answer from the kitchen.

"Out!" Rhys bellowed again to the sleeping couple in the tub before tearing out and grabbing the phone, his heart pounding.

"Rhys, darling? Who was that?" Lady Sterling trilled on the other end of the line. She sounded even more British than usual.

"Um, the . . . delivery guy," Rhys finished lamely.

"Darling, really? Why's he answering the phone?" Lady Sterling asked in confusion. "Ah well, your father and I will be home this evening. I just wanted to let you know. We had a delightful time but then your father's awful brothers got into the old family business and we just couldn't be bothered," she finished.

Rhys cringed. "Sure, Mom," he said automatically, noticing Vince curiously picking up a delicate glass daisy-filled vase from a small end table in the corner.

"Put that back!" Rhys hissed.

"Rhys?" Lady Sterling asked questioningly.

"I'm—I have to go." Rhys rushed to hang up the phone. He wasn't even sure how many people were still *in* the house.

Where there's smoke, there are dirty hippie stoners. . . .

the dawning of a new day

Jack tossed and turned on the organic cotton sheets stretched tightly over the horsehair- and felt-filled California king-size mattress. No matter what, she just couldn't get comfortable. She'd woken up half an hour ago, still in her white Dior gown, but was way too dizzy and nauseated to get up and take it off.

Next to her, J.P. was sprawled out facedown, still wearing his black Harris loafers. So much for passionate sex. She and Avery had ditched the party sometime after midnight and gone to a totally divey bar, where they were the only girls. They'd drunk pitcher after pitcher of crappy beer, done shots with some off-duty cops, and actually had fun. Jack had glanced at her phone around 2 a.m. only to find ten frantic messages from J.P. and his dad, wondering where she was. She'd gotten Avery into a cab and returned to the lofts, where she was immediately whisked away for more photo opportunities, more introductions to totally boring people, and more interviews with dorky cable channels.

And more drinks?

Because she'd disappeared for two hours, Candice and Jeannette wouldn't even let J.P. and Jack out of their sight until 4 a.m., when the party finally wound down. Then, they'd insisted that a NY1 reporter follow them up to the apartment to do a final closing interview. Jack sincerely hoped she didn't sound like a complete idiot on it. Actually, thinking about it, she didn't really give a fuck. She closed her eyes again. Maybe when she opened them, she'd feel less hungover.

Unfortunately, being the face of the Cashman Lofts doesn't come with superpowers.

"Ughhh," J.P. moaned, and flung his arm over Jack's chest in a dreamy haze. Rather than being turned on, Jack was completely turned off. Why couldn't he stick to his side of the bed?

She queasily swung her feet to the ground, practically stepping on Magellan. The little dog gave a low-pitched whine of indignation as she jumped onto the bed.

"Off," Jack hissed, pushing the puppy off the bed. She glanced around the loft. Overnight the hammered-steel countertop in the kitchen had become flooded with gift baskets and bottles of wine. When had that happened?

She wobbled over to the counter and snatched a blueberry muffin from one of the gift baskets. She took a bite. It was totally stale.

"Gorgeous?" J.P. croaked, rolling over and rubbing the sleep from his eyes. His hair was sticking straight up and there was a red pillow indent on the side of his face.

"Morning." Suddenly, Jack had a vision of herself and J.P., fifty years later, still living in the Cashman Lofts. Still waking up to him calling her gorgeous. Still getting way too drunk on champagne and then eating stale muffins the next morning.

"You okay?" J.P. asked, obviously noticing Jack's falling expression.

Jack glanced over at J.P. They'd been together since ninth grade, when they'd met at the Silver and Gold Ball. She'd immediately been attracted to his low-key confidence, the fact that he didn't *need* to prove himself, that he was fine floating through life at an even keel. Jack had loved that about him when they'd started dating, since it offset her tendency toward drama. But now she wanted just a little bit of intrigue. Everything—their entire future—lay before her like a really predictable movie. One that probably wouldn't even air on *Lifetime*, it was so boring. Jack sighed.

"I don't think this is working," she said in a rush, taking another large bite of muffin so she wouldn't have to explain. She didn't even know where that had come from.

J.P.'s mouth dropped open in an O of disbelief.

"I mean, the apartment's not working," Jack added, her mouth still full. "I mean, there's so much pressure and so many people watching us. And it's just a lot of time together, and maybe not in the right way. I mean, have you noticed everyone treats us like we're married?"

"Yeah." J.P. paused. "It's kind of nice."

Jack took a deep breath. "I think we need to slow down. It's great and all that your dad offered me this apartment, but . . . it's too much. I mean, we're only sixteen, you know? I'm moving to my father's place downtown," she said, surprising herself. *Hopefully* her dad would take her in. But she knew it was true: She couldn't stay here anymore.

"I'm going to take a shower. I think I need some alone time." She turned and stalked to the bathroom, hoping he wouldn't be there when she got out.

If he knows what's good for him.

problems solved

Baby was jolted awake by her phone. She was glad she'd had the apartment to herself last night and had spent the entire evening organizing her closet, her photos, and her old notebooks. It was weird, but now that her room was neat, she *did* feel a little more in control. She'd even put some of Avery's clothes back in her closet where they belonged.

"Hello?" she said, her voice cracking.

"Hey! Are you cured yet?" Sydney's raspy voice drawled on the other end of the line.

"I think so?" Baby sat up and surveyed her surroundings, smiling in approval. Now that her room was clean, instead of filled with piles of books, clothes, and random magazines, it actually seemed kind of open and airy.

Good, because it's getting a little cold to sleep on the hammock on the terrace!

"Actually, I *do* feel a lot better. Do you think I could come over and talk to your mom?" she asked, suddenly feeling shy. After all, even though she'd cleaned her closet, Lynn had never officially agreed to take her on as a client. Baby still needed the twenty hours of therapy to stay at Constance.

"She's hosting one of her weird group therapy things this morning, but I guess so." Baby could practically hear Sydney shrugging.

"Great!" Baby quickly flipped her phone shut and flung open her closet door. She'd cleaned so much out that she hardly had anything to wear. Finally, she pulled on a pair of black American Apparel leggings, a flowery dress she'd bought in Barcelona, and a huge heather gray Abercrombie sweater that most likely had once belonged to Owen. She belted the sweater, stuck her feet in a pair of Converse, and ran out the door.

She crossed the park, marveling at how awake the city seemed so early in the morning. The sidewalks were full of families with strollers, kids running in and out of corner delis, and couples sipping coffee and walking hand in hand. Before, so much activity made Baby want to escape. Now it seemed almost exciting, as if she were a part of the city's frantic energy.

She rang the buzzer to Sydney's building and quickly clambered up the stairs, not waiting for the elevator.

"Baby C! Come in, come in, darling!" Lynn flung open the door and ushered her into the living room, where a group of women were gathered. They were crammed onto the worn blue velvet love seat and seated on maroon cushions on the floor. Enya-type music flowed through the room and they were all drawing in sketchbooks.

"I'm doing a group. You want to watch people with problems?" Lynn stage-whispered. Baby glanced over at the women's work. One of the pictures was of a group of elephants standing in the middle of a store that looked sort of like Barneys. She didn't even want to know what the symbolism of that meant.

"We're doing some drawing therapy. Apparently, it's all the rage. I think it's bullshit, but then if it pays the bills, who am I to judge?" Lynn winked conspiratorially. "Besides, if people *feel* like it helps, then it helps. Like I said, not that complicated," she added.

"I don't want to interrupt. I just want to say—"

"Thank you?" Lynn interrupted. "Honey, don't thank me, I didn't do a goddamn thing! All I did was remind you that you're doing fine," she said. "Now, is there anything else I can help you with?"

"Actually . . ." Baby rooted in her lime green Brooklyn Industries messenger bag to find her therapy form. She still had eighteen hours left, and she'd already burned through two different treatment styles. "I'm supposed to go through twenty hours of therapy to stay in school. Do you think you could recommend someone normal . . . or maybe I could see you again?" Baby asked, feeling shy. What if Lynn said no? "I'd pay, of course!" she added.

"Nonsense," Lynn vigorously shook her head. "Give me that form!" She pulled a pen from a chipped coffee mug on the counter and signed the paper with a flourish. "Consider yourself as beautifully and perfectly neurotic as the rest of us!"

"Thanks!" Baby said in disbelief. Just like that, she was *done*! She felt like a huge weight had been lifted from her shoulders.

"Any time, kiddo. Sydney's in her room, hiding out. Why don't you two tear the city up?" Lynn gave Baby's shoulder a squeeze. "Now scoot and let me work my magic!" she said, pushing Baby down the hall and marching her to Sydney's bedroom.

Baby knocked on Sydney's bedroom door. "Hello?"

"Come in!" Sydney was lying on the patchwork quilt on her bed, listening to her iPod and staring up at the ceiling. She was wearing a tiny green corduroy skirt and a black DARE TO SAY THE F WORD—FEMINISM T-shirt.

"I'm cured!" Baby announced, twirling around the room.

"Finally! You've been so lame, you have no idea." Sydney shook her head. "I'm meeting with Webber and his roommates. They're doing this no-pants subway ride. It's what they do to usher in fall. Want to come with?" Sydney grinned devilishly.

"I'm there!" Baby exclaimed.

So what if she liked attention from boys and having fun and never staying in one place? That was her. The real Baby was *back*.

Boys, line up!

reunion

Owen dove into the pool on Saturday morning, enjoying the cold shock of the water against his skin. He quickly pulled to the surface, then loosened up by doing a few quick butterfly strokes before launching into an easy freestyle. He always loved how he could really have time to think, uninterrupted, while he swam. And he definitely had a lot to think about. Namely, that everything about him and Kelsey was wrong. It felt right—physically. But emotionally . . . it was impossible to deny that there was nothing really there. They'd never so much as had a real *conversation*. Once he reached the end of the wall, he pulled himself into a tight turn, only to be stopped by someone pulling on his ankle. What?

Owen stopped and stood in the shallow water.

"Hi!" There, crouching by the end of the pool and looking completely inappropriate in a black sweaterdress, tights, and high-heeled suede boots, was Kelsey.

"Someone brought their cheering section," a male voice boomed.

Owen's stomach sank as he saw Coach jauntily walk out of the locker room, twirling his whistle.

"Sorry, sir!" Owen didn't want Coach to think he was blowing off his captain duties, especially after their conversation on Thursday. He hurriedly pulled himself out of the pool and hustled over to Kelsey. "You shouldn't be here," Owen hissed. The meet didn't start for an hour, but Owen had come early to warm up before the rest of the team arrived. They already hated him, and seeing him with Kelsey would make them even *less* likely to listen to him.

"Well, should we go someplace else?" Kelsey smiled wickedly, then stood on tiptoe to nibble Owen's earlobe. Something about her attitude was so . . . desperate. Had she always been such a nympho?

Um, it takes two to tear each other's clothes off without exchanging names. . . .

"Come here," he muttered, pulling her in the direction of the girls' locker room, knowing it'd be empty. The pool was closed for the meet this morning.

Instead of dented blue lockers, the girls' locker room was filled with pink ones, but it still had the familiar smell of BO and chlorine. Not very romantic, which was probably a good thing. Just to be sure no one would see them, Owen escorted Kelsey inside an equipment closet that housed kickboards and flippers.

Kelsey's eyes widened in lusty delight and she placed her hands against Owen's chest. Could she feel how fast his heart was beating?

"Listen . . . we can't," Owen said heavily, leaning against a soggy mountain of kickboards. He felt like he'd spent more time breaking up with Kelsey in the past few weeks than they'd actually spent having fun together. He wrapped his thumb and index finger easily around one of her wrists.

"Why?" Kelsey asked, her lower lip trembling slightly.

Fuck! Why did this have to be so hard? Why couldn't he just grow some balls and do the honorable thing?

"Kelsey, please." He pulled away. "We can't be together. For real this time." His voice broke slightly. Kelsey's lip was quivering more, and tears were shining in her eyes, just about to fall.

"Why?" she asked again. "I don't understand." She reached to put her arms around Owen's neck.

"It's . . ." Owen paused. "It's this," he said suddenly, pulling away from Kelsey and feeling his entire body relax. It was like they were like magnets. They couldn't be close without touching. But that wasn't the way a relationship worked. A real relationship was about more than physical connection.

Kelsey bit her bottom lip. Owen continued to back away from her. He couldn't touch her.

"Owen?" Kelsey asked, hugging her arms to her chest. She looked like she was about to cry.

Owen wanted to run his hands through her strawberry blond hair and tell her everything would be okay. He wanted to touch the small of her back and pull her to him. But he couldn't. "You deserve to be with someone who really knows you," he said in a rush of words as he practically sprinted out of the equipment room, leaving her standing among a bunch of kickboards. He knew she'd be confused at first, but that eventually she'd get it and be better off. As he left the locker room, he'd never felt more certain that he'd done the right thing.

a is not a gotcha journalist

It was noon on Saturday as Avery burst into the empty *Metropolitan* offices. As soon as she woke up from her drunken haze, one thing was clear: She needed to stop the article on Jack from running. But she didn't know how exactly to do that. It wasn't like she could call and stop the presses. She was hoping she'd come up with some sort of idea now that she was here, but so far all she'd done was sit in the closet.

"Miss Carlyle?" Ticky wavered by on her infamous sparkly Miu Miu pumps, looking surprised and bemused to see her there. "Aren't *you* the eager beaver! I do hope we're not working you too hard. Especially since you were out last night!" she clucked.

"I need to talk to you," Avery squeaked, her mind racing.

"Of course, darling. Come with me to my office." Ticky's brown eyes flashed in concern and she pressed her red-polished fingernails into her arm as she escorted Avery into her opulent office.

"Sit, talk." Ticky gestured to a bright pink chair in front of her desk. Avery felt like she had the one time she was called to the principal's office at Nantucket High. Of course, she'd been called down to be informed she'd won the position of sophomore class vice president, but the initial terror had been the same. And this time, Avery *definitely* wasn't going to get any good news.

"The Jack Laurent and Dick Cashman story can't run," Avery blurted. She felt like she might throw up on Ticky's antique Provençal writing desk, bare except for a typewriter. She concentrated on a framed photo above Ticky's head. It was Ticky, younger but just as skinny, her hair just as high, dancing on a table with Mick Jagger. Avery grimaced. When Ticky was young her antics seemed to have been cool and one-of-a-kind. Not disastrous pseudo-dates with self-centered journalists. "It just can't," Avery added desperately.

"But why?" Ticky asked smoothly. She leaned back in her Eames chair and crossed her skinny arms over her chest. "Avery, you've been a stellar intern. You remind me of me a little bit." She nodded encouragingly. "It's natural to be nervous. It's your first story! And all New York will be talking about it. It's exciting." Ticky smiled benevolently, then waved Avery away with a gnarled hand. "Go, it's the goddamn weekend! I need you to go out there and find more *stories*. It's the only way to get over this hump," Ticky said grandly.

"Um, thank you." Avery tried to get her footing back. "It's just . . . the story about Jack . . . It's not . . ." She sighed heavily. What could she say? *Jack and I both sort of hated acting like adults at the party and instead of going through with the interview decided to drink crappy beer at a dive bar?*

"Wait." Ticky pulled the large proof off her inbox and studied it. Right now, it was just waiting for her swirling initials in her signature Montblanc pen with purple ink. She pushed her delicate Prada reading glasses up on the bridge of her beaklike nose and looked up sharply. "She's not having an affair with that old man," Ticky said flatly. Avery nodded in relief.

"I should have said something before. You can fire me if you want, but you have to pull the story. It's just not true. It's not true," Avery said again, feeling even more sure that the champagne and beer swirling in her stomach from last night was going to make an unwelcome cameo appearance very soon. She needed to get out.

"I'm sorry!" Avery squeaked as she fled the room and ran into the bathroom. She splashed cold water on her face. In the mirror, she looked red and blotchy and very, very tired. Not *Metropolitan* material at all. She left the bathroom and stalked over to her desk, grabbing one issue of the magazine and stuffing it into her cranberry-colored Marc Jacobs bag. Scarlett Johansson was on the cover, wearing a plaid Prada skirt and looking in control and confident. Unlike Avery.

Just then, she heard the familiar sound of Ticky's heels clicking across the tiled floor. Great. Now she'd *really* lay into Avery. Avery squared her shoulders, sort of wishing she'd thrown up in the bathroom before.

"Avery?" Ticky's voice wavered as she got closer.

"Here," Avery squeaked.

"Dear, what are you doing?" Ticky looked at the bare desk. "You're acting like my goddamn ex-husband. One bitchy moment from me and he'd be packing his stuff. Then, when I actually *did* kick him out, that bastard seemed so surprised!" Ticky shook her head bemusedly. Avery smiled politely.

"You're right. Let's kill the story. It's based on a salacious rumor, which is simply not *Metropolitan*. Do you agree?" Avery nodded, dumbfounded. She wasn't in trouble? "I shouldn't have put you with James. Although you certainly held your own with him," Ticky mused. "Now, let's get you working on a *real* story. What do you want to do?"

Avery thought. She tried to imagine running around with a tiny tape recorder, asking people what they were wearing and how they liked the party, or even some of the more hard-core questions *Metropolitan* liked to ask, like their worst childhood memory or their biggest fear. But she couldn't. In every single image she had of her ideal New York life, *she* was the one in the spotlight, answering questions.

"Actually . . ." Avery shook her head. Before, all she'd wanted was for Ticky to accept her and say she was *Metropolitan* material, as if that'd be her magical key to New York. But it wasn't really that simple. She didn't want to become like McKenna or Gemma, desperately clawing their way to the top. "You've always been a role model to me, especially after my grandmother passed away," Avery began shyly. "But I just don't think this is the right industry for me," she said, hoping Ticky wouldn't be offended or ask her to explain further.

Surprisingly, Ticky nodded thoughtfully. "I'd like to think you'd reconsider in a few years. You've cut your teeth already. And once you have a taste for magazines, as bitter as it is, you'll always crave more. Besides, God knows this industry needs some people with real class. I can't do it alone," Ticky said ruefully. She rested her garishly polished red fingernails lightly on Avery's arm. "But guess what? For your work and honesty, I'm going to offer you the Ticky special. *Metropolitan* won't write anything nasty about you. Unless you want it, kiddo. Deal?"

Avery beamed, hardly able to believe what she was hearing. Ticky had the ultimate say in what was, and what was not, said about practically everyone in the city. It was a promise that she mattered. Just like her grandmother.

"I don't know how I can thank you," Avery began earnestly.

"Just keep this city interesting." Ticky winked and turned to go.

Avery leaned down and picked up one of the ridiculous sequins that had become detached from her pumps. "Wait!"

Ticky turned mid-step, balancing on one foot like an underfed flamingo.

"You dropped this," Avery explained shyly, holding out the sequin.

"Keep it!" Ticky crowed. Even though it was sort of sentimental, Avery carefully shoved it in the never-used change purse pocket of her black Prada wallet.

Well, it's not like she was expecting a Pulitzer.

Avery sighed in relief and headed toward the elevator. She was looking forward to her last journey to the lobby of the Dennen building.

As the elevator doors opened, she found herself face-to-face with James. He wore blue checked shirt, a plaid bow tie, and a herringbone jacket. Yesterday, Avery would have thought he looked urbane and cool. Today, he just looked like he was trying too hard.

"Oh good, pet, you're here!" he exclaimed, pulling her over and kissing her on both cheeks. Avery stood stiffly. *Pet?* "I can't wait to hear your stories, even though I couldn't find you at all when I was ready to go. You missed a lot," he warned.

"No, you did," Avery countered smoothly. She studied James curiously. She couldn't believe that she'd fallen for the accent and the job title when all he was was a self-obsessed jerk with a really lame personal shopper. "But let me catch you up to speed: I'm not working here anymore. And the profile isn't running, because *Metropolitan* doesn't do salacious rumor mongering. Can't wait to read your next story!" she called over her shoulder, just before she exited through the revolving doors.

r remembers some house rules

"I'll invite you over for a party next time," Lucas said seriously as he took a long drag of a joint. He blew the smoke upward, toward the cathedral-like wood-beamed foyer of the Sterling town house. Lisa, Vince, and five or six other kids Rhys had never seen before were circled around him as if he were their new guru, each holding tomatoes in their hands.

"Thanks," Rhys said tightly. "Look, man, hope there's no hard feelings, but you guys have to go." *Now.* He opened the large heavy oak door. "I'll see you around," he croaked. Yeah right. As if he'd ever hang out with the dirty, smelly kids who'd almost ruined his life.

"I'm going to use these fuckers for my pasta sauce. These heirloom tomatoes are to die for," Lucas mused, as if he were Mario Batali rather than a super-stoned teenager. He picked up two of the tomatoes and began throwing them in the air in a lame attempt at juggling. Rhys felt his heart speed up. Maybe be was about to have a heart attack. Could pot do that to someone?

"Anyway, man, peace. Thanks for the good times," Lucas finally said, once it was obvious Rhys wasn't going to respond.

One by one, the other hippies nodded as they followed Lucas out the door.

Bye-bye, never come back!

Rhys bolted up the winding stairs to his parents' master suite two at a time, ready to survey the damage. He had a pounding headache, and even though he'd brushed his teeth, his mouth still tasted as if he'd licked the entire floor of the locker room at St. Jude's. He was never going to smoke or drink again. Once his parents found out what had happened, he'd never be allowed to go out again anyway, so it would work out perfectly.

He opened the door of his parents' suite, relieved when he didn't see any tomatoes, joints, or osetra caviar tins littering the floor. Maybe he could meet his parents at the door when they arrived, blindfold them, and escort them to their bedroom so he'd have time to clean?

Great idea!

He collapsed on the bed on his back, kneading his temples. He just needed a moment before he figured out a plan. There had to be some disaster-fixing Saturday morning cleaning service, right? He looked up at the ceiling, feeling lonelier than ever. The house was a shithole. He was a loser. And he'd bitched out Owen.

Not knowing what else to do, he pulled his swim bag out of the hall closet and jogged over to the Ninety-second Street Y. It was the last thing he should be doing right now, and yet . . . it was also the first. He needed to feel the water around him, to actually put some effort into something. He wanted to care, instead of just smoking his way through life.

"Coach?" he asked, making his way over to the makeshift office in the locker room. He was going to apologize and see if Coach would let him back. It was a long shot, but he had to try it.

"Sterling!" Coach clapped his hand on his back. "You smell." He wrinkled his nose. "Anyway, get your banana hammock on and get in the water. You're swimming the hundred fly. Goddamn Chadwick has chicken pox. What a pussy!" Coach shook his head with annoyance. While Rhys felt bad for the super-skinny, super-awkward freshman, he could barely conceal a grin.

When his event was called, Rhys walked to the blocks as if in a dream. He noticed Owen in the lane next to him, a shocked expression spreading on his face once he realized he was swimming with Rhys. Rhys rolled his shoulders back, trying to loosen up. He'd talk to Owen later. Right now, it was just him and the water.

Once he dove in, he was surprised at how easy it was to find his rhythm in the pool. A long time ago, he used to think the butterfly was like sex—or like sex would be, if he'd ever had it. Now, he just felt the power, the control. After days of smoking and eating greasy food, it felt good to banish the laziness from his body and actually use his muscles again. Feeling a final surge of energy, he slammed into the wall.

"You won, buddy!" Owen was in the next lane, pulling off his maroon swim cap and dunking his head under the heavily chlorinated water. He held out a hand. "Seriously great job, man!"

Rhys could barely conceal a grin.

"It's over," Owen whispered as they pulled themselves out of the pool. "I broke up with her."

What? Did Owen mean he and Kelsey were done? Before, Rhys would have wanted to jump up and down in happiness. Now, he just felt . . . *fine*. Like he couldn't care either way. Everything was falling into place, but even if it hadn't been, he knew he'd be okay.

And he thought he didn't learn anything from his hippie friends!

Rhys walked toward the locker room, feeling ridiculously happy and wanting to wave at everyone sitting on the rickety metal bleachers. There were a lot of girls there. Why had he never noticed before? One with freckles and long bangs that almost covered her eyes waved at him, mouthing *good job* in his direction.

Coach clapped his hand on Rhys's back. "Awesome job, my man! We won!" He pumped Rhys's hand enthusiastically. "But you've got to get used to the chlorine again. Your eyes are all red."

Right. The chlorine.

"So, are you back?" Coach asked, knitting his brows together. "Because if you are, then I'll need to have a chat with you and Carlyle."

"No need, sir." Owen caught up to them and opened the wooden door of the locker room, allowing Rhys to pass. "I want Rhys to take back the captainship. If he'll have it."

Rhys surveyed the locker room, where the guys were all busily getting dressed. The dented blue lockers looked the same as ever, but Rhys felt a huge wave of nostalgia. He locked eyes with Owen, who simply nodded in a way that said, *Take it, it's yours.* Finally, he nodded.

"All right." Coach's face cracked into a huge grin. "And I have to say, that was very manly of you, Carlyle. All for one, and all that. I'm proud of you men!"

"Thanks, sir," Hugh called back angelically. He leaned over and rifled through his maroon swim bag, pulling out a slightly crushed-looking black pirate's hat. He placed it on Rhys's head, and the whole team started cheering.

When everyone had showered and changed, Owen and Rhys

found themselves standing next to each other again. "Hey man," Rhys began, wanting to thank Owen for Kelsey and the captainship and just about everything, when his phone rang. He pulled out his black iPhone. An unfamiliar number flashed across the screen. "Hello?" he asked curiously.

"Rhys, Anka's been playing the most absurd trick on me this morning!" The clipped voice of Lady Sterling emanated from the phone. She sounded hysterical, like the time on *Tea with Lady Sterling* when they'd invited all the dogs from the Westminster Dog Show and the Best in Show dog had peed on Lady Sterling's pink Chanel suit. "She called to say that there was a party at the house last night. The house is in quite a state, and she's not even talking to me, she's so angry!" Lady Sterling fretted.

Rhys collapsed heavily against the worn wooden bench of the locker room, resting his elbows on his knees. Fuck. This wasn't good. His head hurt.

"Rhys?" Lady Sterling's voice rose an octave. It felt like someone was taking an ice pick directly to his brain.

"You're in *trouble*!" Hugh mouthed.

"Why did Anka say my heirloom tomatoes were taking a swim in the pool!" Lady Sterling screeched.

"It's . . . uh, bad connection," Rhys said brilliantly. "You're breaking up." He pressed end call, then hastily turned the phone off. When his parents got home today and saw that Anka was telling the truth, he was going to be in for it. "Know a good cleaning service?" Rhys smiled lopsidedly at Owen. He *really* hoped his parents didn't disown him.

"I do!" Hugh swaggered over. "What are you looking at? Puke stains, fingerprints or minor burns?" He whipped out his phone and squinted seriously at the screen.

Any tomato juice–removing specialists?

"Which do you recommend?" Rhys asked. Of course Hugh would know. His parents spent most of their time on their yacht, so Hugh's town house had been the de facto party house since middle school.

Once Hugh had given Rhys a full analysis of his various post–party house rehab services, Rhys made a few calls. Immediately, he felt a bit better. But he still didn't want to go home. "My mom's going to have my ass," he sighed to Owen.

"So give her a little time to cool off. Just come stay at my place," Owen offered shyly.

"Could I really?" Rhys asked excitedly.

Bromance, part deux?

uptown girl

Jack looked up at the bay window of the austere, four-story nineteenth-century Greek Revival town house on Bank Street that belonged to her father. Inside, she could just make out the dining room, and the white shock of her father's hair presiding over the dinner table. After she told J.P. she couldn't stay at the lofts any-more, she'd slowly packed up her belongings and made her way to the West Village. She hadn't called her dad first, because it would just have been too awkward to explain the whole situation over the phone. The last thing she wanted to do was beg her dad to take her in. She'd hoped that once she got here and he saw her bags, he'd understand and take her to the guest room, no questions asked.

But now that she was here, watching her happy stepfamily eat dinner through the bay window, she couldn't go in. She couldn't face ringing the doorbell and admitting that her dad was right, she needed help. She couldn't deal with her twin stepbrat sisters, or her only-eight-years-older stepmother, Rebecca.

She plopped down on the steps, feeling the cold seep through her Citizen skinny jeans. She couldn't believe she'd moved out of the Cashman Lofts.

Jack pulled out her cell, wondering whom she could call. There was always Genevieve, but her apartment was positively tiny and her mom, a former actress who now starred exclusively on Lifetime Television dramas, was incredibly loud and embarrassing. Still, beggars couldn't be choosers. Just as Jack was debating whether she could live with a histrionic and self-obsessed mom who wasn't *related* to her, her phone rang.

"Um, hi?" Jack began, trying to whisper. The last thing she wanted was one of the nosy stepbrats to peek out the window and see her.

"Hey, it's Avery." Avery's voice always sounded perky, like she'd drunk three Dean & Deluca lattes in a row. How come *Avery* didn't feel as hungover as she did?

"How are you?" Jack asked suspiciously. She still couldn't believe they'd ditched the lofts party to hang out with a bunch of off-duty cops at a dive bar last night. Still, it had been pretty fun.

"Good. A little hungover," Avery giggled easily into the phone. Jack imagined Avery in her gorgeous Fifth Avenue penthouse apartment. She suddenly felt very small and lonely. "How are you surviving at the lofts?"

"Um." Jack paused. "I actually moved out. It was just . . ." Just what? Too nice? Too elegant? "It wasn't working." There. She said it. Somehow, once the words tumbled out, Jack fully realized what she'd done. She'd moved out of the most awesome apartment she'd probably ever live in. She'd practically rejected J.P., although technically they were still together. She'd fucked up her own goddamn life.

Suddenly, a sob began working its way up her chest, but she didn't want to lose control over the phone. Instead, she twisted an auburn strand of hair around her index finger, sticking the ends in her mouth. It was a gross habit, one she only engaged in when she was under extreme emotional duress. But it wasn't like Avery could see her.

"That's too bad." Avery sounded like she really meant it. "Do you want to come over?" Avery offered in such a small voice, at first Jack thought she hadn't heard properly. "I'm just hanging out," Avery added uncertainly.

"Sure," Jack said slowly. "But I have a lot of stuff with me. . . ." She gazed down at the two slightly battered Louis Vuitton steamer trunks propped against the concrete fish-patterned planters at the foot of the steps.

"Whatever, there's plenty of room. Seriously, stay as long as you want. It'll be fun." Avery sounded so sincere and sweet, but instead of being annoyed by it, Jack was almost . . . touched.

"Well, I guess I could stop by," Jack said matter-of-factly, still sucking on the just-trimmed ends of her auburn hair. She slid off her trunk and dragged it over to Seventh Avenue. Immediately, a cabbie stopped on the corner.

"Seventy-second and Fifth," Jack rattled off. The cabbie nodded, opened the trunk of the car, hoisted her trunks inside, and slammed it closed.

"I'll take you to where you belong," the cabbie said gallantly. Jack nodded as she slid onto the black vinyl seats of the cab and shut the door. She wasn't quite sure where she belonged, but at least she knew her first stop.

where love is just a glance away . . .

"I made carob bars!" Edie wandered onto the moonlit terrace, trailed by a tall, broad-shouldered man in jeans and a button-down. He was in his mid-forties with salt-and-pepper hair, and looked shockingly normal next to Edie in her flowing maxidress and Princess Leia buns.

"Thanks!" Avery called from her perch on Baby's hammock, where she and Jack were sitting in companionable silence, flipping through magazines and listening to Avery's iPod, which was playing a steady stream of John Mayer and Jason Mraz. Owen and his friend Rhys were having an earnest discussion on a pine bench, just out of earshot, and Baby was coming out as soon as she finished cleaning her closet or whatever she was doing in her room. Avery felt surprisingly content. After last night, it was nice to just relax and not have to worry about trying to impress anyone.

"Anyone?" Edie asked hopefully, proffering the plate into the chilly night air. Once she realized there were no takers, Edie placed the plate on the terra-cotta floor and absentmindedly ruffled Jack's auburn hair.

"Hi," Jack said uncomfortably. She wasn't 100 percent sure Edie was aware she wasn't a Carlyle.

"Hello, darling! You're the lovely girl who was here for our dinner party a few weeks back!"

"That's me!" Jack smiled politely, trying to sound enthusiastic. Back when she'd been pretending to date Owen, she'd been over to the Carlyle penthouse and experienced the world's weirdest intergenerational dinner party.

"Well, we're not going to *bother* you chickadees! We're just taking in the night air!" Edie said, knitting her eyebrows together as if affronted that her adolescent children didn't want to hang out with her. Behind her, Remington shuffled nervously, smiling politely. "Anyway, Remington was telling me about this *fantastic* all-night poetry salon in the Village. So we're going to go to that. I *was* going to invite you to come." Edie raised her eyebrow expectantly.

"That's okay!" Avery said quickly. She was *not* about to tag along on her mom's all-night date. How serious was Edie getting with this guy, anyway? She raised an eyebrow, surveying Remington. He was kind of handsome, actually, for someone her mom's age, and way more normal-seeming than anyone she would have imagined winding up at her mom's art collaborative. *Interesting*. Now that she was done at *Metropolitan*, at least she'd have time to keep tabs on her family.

And turn it into a best-selling novel?

"Have it your way." Edie shook her head sadly, causing her heavy wooden necklace to click together loudly. "You kids need to learn to live!" she added. Remington nodded in agreement, picking up the platter of carob bars and following Edie through the French doors and back into the house.

"Sorry about that." Avery shrugged and pulled out the unopened Corona she'd halfheartedly tried to obscure behind a planter. "Want one?"

"Sure." Jack took the cold bottle. Instead of opening it, she held it against her head, still trying to get rid of her headache. Surprisingly, she felt better now that she was hanging out at the Carlyles', even though she was homeless and not sure about her boyfriend anymore. The moon hung over Central Park perfectly, round and full, almost like a set piece. The terrace, with its sweeping view of the park and the fog that was clinging to all the tops of the buildings, felt almost magical.

"Hey!" Baby clattered through the French doors, wearing a pair of Citizen jeans that actually fit her, along with a cool Marc Jacobs–style purple tunic. She still looked hippieish, but less bag lady. "Oh, you're here." Baby announced it like a fact, staring at Jack with her wide brown eyes. "And so is *he*." Jack followed Baby's gaze over to the corner of the terrace, where Owen and his friend Rhys were sitting side by side on a pine bench, looking over Central Park. In the almost-darkness, Jack could just make out Owen's handsome, athletic silhouette. He and Rhys kept bumping their fists together and laughing, involved in some sort of private guy-bonding moment.

"Guys!" Avery called bossily over to them. What could they *possibly* be up to?

"What?" Owen and Rhys lumbered over together.

"We need more drinks." Avery smiled. That was the great thing about having an older brother.

Three minutes older. Makes such a big difference.

Just then, the iPod switched from Avery's party mix to a slower song.

"Oops!" Avery quickly picked up her iPod, embarrassed. It was some cheesy Frank Sinatra song she only listened to by herself.

"'Strangers in the Night,'" Rhys said. "Leave it on—I like it."

"Really?" Avery arched an eyebrow. Rhys looked so athletic and masculine, she couldn't imagine him listening to dorky Frank Sinatra songs.

"Yeah." Rhys shrugged. Avery scooted over a bit on the hammock to see if Rhys would sit down. "I'm Avery. We've never officially met."

"Rhys." Rhys stuck his hand out. Avery took it and shook, then leaned back against the hammock.

"Anyone need anything from inside?" Owen asked. Baby shook her head. Avery shook hers as well, then pulled her dark purple Milly sweater closer around her shoulders.

"I'll come with you!" Jack said, quickly standing up and following Owen inside.

"You cold?" Rhys asked, holding out his royal blue Ralph Lauren letterman-style sweater as an offering.

"Thanks." Avery took it shyly and wrapped it around her shoulders. It smelled like Ralph Lauren Romance with a slight trace of smoke. She was surprised at how much she liked the smell, and how much she liked that Rhys sat down next to her.

In the corner, Avery noticed Baby sitting cross-legged, petting Rothko and looking perfectly content. Avery sighed and scooted a little bit closer toward Rhys. He smiled back at her. Somewhere inside, she could hear Jack's laughter, followed by Owen's dorky-sounding chuckle. He only laughed like that when he was trying to impress someone.

"Strangers in the Night" continued to play and Avery took a deep breath of the crisp fall air. No one was fighting or gossiping or making out or crying. It was so unexpected and weird and beautiful.

Only in New York!

gossipgirl.net

Disclaimer: All the real names of places, people, and events have been altered or abbreviated to protect the innocent. Namely, me.

topics   sightings   your e-mail   post a question

hey people!

You know how everyone always bemoans the day in late October when suddenly Balthazar stops setting up al fresco tables, when the garden at Vespa on Second is locked, and when the rooftop bar at the Maritime only opens for parties? It's time to stop whining and realize that the cold just means the party has moved to private rooftops—as exemplified by a gathering occurring at a certain penthouse on Seventy-second and Fifth. And we all know the best thing about hanging out in the great outdoors in mixed company as the temperature dips: Cuddling is practically required.

So, is that why **A** and **R** were swooning over Sinatra? And why did **O** suddenly have to go help **J** unpack into her new abode? And why was **B** spotted solo, with only her cat for company? It's a cliché, but this is the city that never sleeps . . . so what happens when sleeping arrangements are all under one roof?

your e-mail

Dear GG,
So, we had this intern at the magazine I work at. She was only there for like a week, but now she's all our editor in chief can talk about. She always compares me to her. What should I do?
—writergrrrrl

239

a: Dear WG,
Why don't you showcase your talents by writing *about* her? Sometimes you have to think outside the cube!
—GG

q: Dear Gossip Girl,
Will u please date me?
—Desperate

a: Dear Desperate,
Rule number one: Don't ever *say* you're desperate. As for me, unfortunately, I only donate to *established* charities.
—GG

Sometimes, the best thing to do on a chilly Saturday night is to get your beauty rest, then gloat at your hungover friends when you meet for Sunday brunch at Sarabeth's. Besides, I have a few questions of my own I need to sleep on:

What will happen when **R** faces the wrath of **Lady S** when she realizes her "Terrific Tomatoes" show is ruined? Will it be off to boarding school in the UK for our favorite reformed stoner? Now that **B** has given up castoffs in favor of streamlining, what can we expect to see from her? Has **A** met her Emily Post protocol–perfect opposite? Will **A** and **J**'s friendship *really* last? The sun'll come out tomorrow . . . and we'll see what else does. Remember, in the cold light of day, nothing stays secret. At least not when I'm around.

You know you love me,

gossip girl

Spotted back in NYC:
Blair, **S**erena,
Nate, and **C**huck

And guess who will be there to
whisper all their juicy secrets?

i will always love you

a gossip girl
novel

An all-new special hardcover edition,
featuring the original cast.

Coming November 2009.

poppy

www.pickapoppy.com

Spotted: **B, S, N, D** and **Little J**
on Limited Collector's Editions of the #1 bestselling Gossip Girl novels that inspired the CW's hit show.

Each edition includes an exclusive poster on the reverse side of the jacket featuring a gorgeous, frame-worthy image from the show.

Add style and scandal to your library.
Collect all twelve!

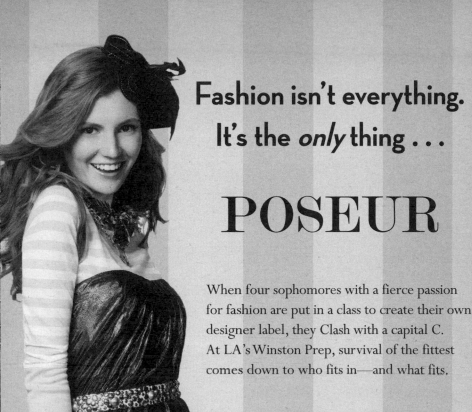

Fashion isn't everything.
It's the *only* thing . . .

POSEUR

When four sophomores with a fierce passion for fashion are put in a class to create their own designer label, they Clash with a capital C. At LA's Winston Prep, survival of the fittest comes down to who fits in—and what fits.

POSEUR

The Good, the Fab and the Ugly

Petty in Pink (coming July 2009)

Welcome to Poppy.

A poppy is a beautiful blooming red flower
(like the one on the spine of this book). It is also
the name of the home of your favorite series.

Poppy takes the real world and makes it
a little funnier, a little more fabulous.

Poppy novels are wild, witty, and inspiring.
They were written just for you.

So sit back, get comfy, and pick a Poppy.

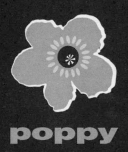

poppy

www.pickapoppy.com